"That man?" The ship's officer hesitated. Julie wondered why.

"That man is Mark Sefton. We've had him with us on several trips."

"I suppose his job takes him abroad a lot," Julie said. "I think someone mentioned that he is an insurance investigator."

"Not Sefton," the officer said, sounding like a man who is sure of his facts.

As though aware that he was being discussed, Mark Sefton turned his head and looked directly at Julie. She sustained the scrutiny of those brilliant eyes for a moment, feeling that she was being X-rayed, and then her lashes dropped, her cheeks burned.

WHO COULD HE BE?

EMILIE LORING
NO TIME
FOR LOVE

A NATIONAL GENERAL COMPANY

NO TIME FOR LOVE
*A Bantam Book / published by arrangement with
Little, Brown and Company*

PRINTING HISTORY
Little, Brown edition published August 1970
Bantam edition published October 1972
2nd printing
3rd printing

*Bantam Books are published by Bantam Books, Inc., a National
General company. Its trade-mark, consisting of the words "Bantam
Books" and the portrayal of a bantam, is registered in the United
States Patent Office and in other countries. Marca Registrada.
Bantam Books, Inc., 666 Fifth Avenue, New York, N.Y. 10019.*

PRINTED IN THE UNITED STATES OF AMERICA

I

It was on June twenty-fourth that the story broke about the jewel robbery. Later, Julie was to remember that it was the only thing that had ever successfully stopped Bert Wilson short in the middle of a proposal. He had proposed to her in the midst of a thunderstorm (hoping, he told her, that sheer terror would make her turn to him); on a dance floor (only a heart of stone would be unmoved by that melting music); hanging on the side of a mountain waiting for the man at the head of the rope to signal that they could move up (only a monster would fail to turn to the manly arms waiting to protect her).

Under these and half a dozen other unlikely conditions Julie had laughingly rejected his proposals, and each time Bert had mildly but firmly assured her that he would continue to ask her to marry him until she accepted.

"It's that constant dripping that wears away the stone and if there was ever a stone, it's what you use for a heart."

And Julie, in these romantic situations, would remind him calmly that he had overparked and would have to pay a fine or that hot soup wouldn't make his sensitive tooth hurt if he had sense enough to go to a dentist.

"To think," Bert would groan, "that I had to fall in love with a girl who is about as romantic as a—a cabbage."

"If that's what you think, you're cured," she told him cheerfully.

"No, only when, in my eyes, you really resemble a cabbage will I be cured. What is it about you?" he demanded rather resentfully. "What makes me so dizzy

1

that I don't know whether I'm on my head or my heels?
This thing has gone on—how long? Since you were
fourteen and had braces on your teeth. And very plain
you were then, I can tell you. So what's so wonderful
about you?"

She leaned back, her face alight with laughter.
" 'Item,' " she quoted, " 'two lips indifferent red; item,
two gray eyes, with lids to them; item, one neck, one
chin, and so forth.' "

Bert grinned. Julie Bryce had known him for nine
years, a lanky, homely redhead with a wonderful sense
of humor, a dogged individualism, a sense of justice, and
an integrity that nothing could shake. He had scolded
her and been patient with her; he had laughed at her
and praised her; he had stood by, quietly though sometimes wistfully, and let other boys, whose pockets were
better lined, escort her to dances and games and theaters. And all the time he had loved her.

Now his eyes twinkled as he answered her. "That is
Shakespeare's Olivia you are describing, my girl. Except
that she was another hard-hearted wench, it doesn't
apply to you. Your eyes are brown with yellow flecks in
them when you laugh. Your hair is light brown with gold
lights when the sun strikes it. Your eyelashes are long
enough to sweep the floor—and darn it, if they don't
have a sooty look as though that were just what they've
been doing! Your complexion makes a mockery of anything the famous Sobelli cosmetics can produce. You are
beautiful and maddening, headstrong and tantalizing,
and, if I had the sense I was born with, I'd stop loving
you this minute. The trouble is that I can't."

For all the lightness in his voice, his eyes were serious.
Then his big mouth curled in an infectious smile. "All
right, honey, not another word. That is, until next time.
But I might remind you of my exceptional qualifications
as a husband so you can bear them in mind. We start
first with my unique charm, my—"

And that was when Julie flicked on the car radio. She
wanted to stop him. Her affection for him was so deep
that she could not bear the realization of how much
unhappiness she caused him. And yet—and yet—fine as
he was, she did not love him.

Some months earlier, when she had been firmer than usual in her rejection, he had asked her, "What kind of man are you looking for, Julie?"

"I don't know, but I'll recognize him when I see him."

"A glamour guy?"

She shook her head.

"A Tarzan who can swing from trees? A Wall Street wizard? A Greek magnate who owns half the earth? A movie star?"

She shook her head again. "It won't be money that counts," she had been deeply serious for once as she tried to explain her own values, her own dreams, "or a man who wants power for its own sake. I'm not that empty-headed. And I don't think it would be good looks; at least unless he has a lot more than that to recommend him."

"Now those are cheering comments," Bert had said with his attractive grin. "I know a character who just fits the specifications, especially about the qualities he doesn't have to have. You'd better change your mind, Julie, and take me. For better for worse. Join the deserving poor before that plush life ruins you."

"It won't ruin me," she had told him soberly. "Aunt Georgia may live in a lavish sort of way but she is simple at heart and she has great courage. Look at the way she built her business after Uncle Dino died. She was terribly in love with him, but instead of feeling sorry for herself, she built a whole new life and created one of the most successful cosmetic businesses in the world."

"Is it?" Bert had asked queerly.

Julie's big eyes seemed even bigger when she opened them wide in surprise. "Well, of course."

"There's no 'of course' about it, Julie, my love. Even in my humble position in the newspaper world, as chief emptier of wastebaskets, I hear things. Rumors get around. There is one rumor I've been hearing lately and that is that Sobelli Cosmetics, Inc., is on the verge of bankruptcy."

Julie was stunned and then angry. "That's not true! The business is flourishing. Why, Aunt Georgia was talking not long ago about opening new shops in Los Angeles and Dallas and Chicago. And you know she already has famous shops in Florence, Rome, Paris, London and New York, as well as the headquarters here and the factory in New Jersey."

"Maybe the business is as sound as you say." Bert remained dubious. "But I'll have to admit that is not the impression that is going around. Far from it. And if your aunt sets up a new shop anywhere in the next six months, I will buy you an oversized ice-cream cone, and you can't be fairer than that."

"Don't let Aunt Georgia hear you talk like that," Julie had warned him. "Her business has become husband and family to her. She'd fight like a tigress for it."

"A woman needs more than that," Bert said, his eyes sober. "You've got to have more to live with than a—a cash register."

"You don't understand Aunt Georgia," Julie said, hot in the defense of the woman who had looked after her most of her life, given her a home and education and affection and tried unsuccessfully to establish her in a social career. This was the only time when Julie balked. While her aunt worked, she had no intention of spending her life going to parties and giving them, playing instead of working. The situation had ended in a draw that was unsatisfactory to both of them. Julie rejected a debut and the social life to follow. Her aunt remained firm in the decision not to take her into the cosmetic business.

"Perhaps not," Bert said amiably. "But to me she is just a beautiful woman who is all veneer. Under that smooth surface she is hard as nails."

"No, it is only on the surface and in her profession that she appears so—so sort of lacquered and unreal. That is because she had to build a kind of façade when she was terribly hurt. She married Prince Dino Sobelli for love, not for his title and position, whatever people may say, and when he died, absolutely impoverished, she needed something to fill up her life and, what's more, she wanted money to give me the kind of life she thought I would choose for myself. So she developed this business and made it a terrific success. And she hasn't been a cash register to me. She has been wonderful and generous and kind."

Bert turned to smile at the earnest face. "Wonderful, maybe. Kind, maybe. Generous? Not from what I hear. If she is so darned generous, so lavish in her spending, why didn't she ever repair her husband's old palace in Florence, deeply devoted to his memory as she claims to be? Way I hear it, the place is falling to pieces from neglect. Rumor says that your Aunt Georgia is just plain tight-fisted."

"She is not!" Julie had red spots of anger in her cheeks.

"Then she must be broke. You can't have it both ways."

That had been some weeks ago, and they had parted in smoldering anger. Bert did not have red hair for nothing and he knew that his sources of information were reliable. To him it seemed that Julie's loyalty to her aunt blinded her. On her part, Julie, aware of her heavy debt of gratitude to her aunt and trusting in the appearances of success and wealth, felt that he had been misled and that he was being unjust.

Now, some weeks after their original quarrel, they were returning from a weekend in Westchester. Julie had been staying at her aunt's big house, luxuriating mornings in the swimming pool and magnificence of the rose garden, playing tennis afternoons at the country club, and dancing at night. Bert Wilson, whose family could not afford country-club dues, had spent his time mowing the lawn and trimming bushes at his father's modest house.

Julie had suggested that she call for him in her aunt's Lincoln and that he drive them both back to New York, away from the coolness of the country and into the damp smothering discomfort of an early heat wave. There was no reason why Julie could not have remained at the country house, but she had never given up hope that someday her aunt would change her mind and let her train for the business.

Since the time of their quarrel about the solvency of Sobelli Cosmetics, Inc., Julie had seen little of Bert. In her loyalty to her aunt she had intended to make him aware of her displeasure. But now, as always in their arguments, from the time when they were children, they were friends again, and Bert was just launching into a mock-serious account of his qualifications as a husband when the radio, which Julie had turned on in the hope of interrupting him, began to give the news of the day. War, politics, housing, taxes, weather went their gloomy way. Then Julie raised her head, lips parted in stunned surprise and shock.

"Police are still investigating the theft of jewelry amounting to nearly a quarter of a million dollars from the Park Avenue town house of Princess Sobelli, president and founder of Sobelli Cosmetics, Inc. So far no clue as to the identity of the thief has been found nor has anyone learned how he managed to enter the house, which is carefully locked at all times, and where a staff of five servants is employed, all of whom were on the premises at the time when the theft is assumed to have occurred, between eight and eleven last night."

"Oh," Julie gasped, "how awful! Poor Aunt Georgia! How could it possibly have happened? A quarter of a million dollars! I had no idea her jewelry was so valuable. I wonder why she didn't call me last night and tell me?"

In her usual eager way she chattered on, speculating about how the theft could have occurred, how anyone could have learned where the jewelry was kept, whether any of the servants could have been involved. Absently she snapped off the radio, cutting off a popular song, and in the silence that followed she realized for the first time that Bert had not spoken since the news had been announced. She turned to him in some surprise, for he was nothing if not vocal, saw the grim set of his lips, which were made for smiling; the intentness of the eyes that usually mocked her so gently.

"Why did your aunt keep so much jewelry in the house instead of in a bank vault?" he asked. "It sounds like absolute madness."

"I don't know why," Julie admitted. "About a month ago she removed all her jewelry from her safety-deposit box at the bank and had a safe designed and built by a specialist into the side of her bed. Not even the house-maids could have guessed that it was there. The whole thing was done when the house was being repainted and decorated in May and the servants were away."

"But someone must have known," Bert persisted. "You see that, don't you?"

"I don't think it could be possible," Julie admitted. "Aunt Georgia told no one but me and the man who installed the safe."

"It couldn't have happened, Julie."

"What do you mean?"

"No thief got into that house, locked up and guarded as it was, and discovered by sheer chance a safe concealed in as unlikely place as the side of a bed, during the only three hours when the bedroom was sure to be unoccupied. It's not possible."

"You mean that there was an informer who told the thief where to look? But no one knew except me and I certainly didn't tell anyone. Even you."

"No, I don't mean that."

"Then I don't understand what in the world you are getting at with that mysterious manner of yours."

There was a long time when Bert did not answer. Then he said, "You aren't going to like this, honey. You aren't going to like it at all. But just give a guy a break, will you? Listen to me, as the lawyers say, 'without prejudice.'"

"Of course." She was bewildered and a little disturbed by his manner.

"All right then. I've been telling you for weeks that rumors are circulating about the Sobelli Cosmetics outfit, indicating that it is on the rocks, that your aunt is stony broke."

"But—"

"You still don't get it, do you? Here it is in a nutshell. It is my personal belief that the theft never happened."

"Never—" The soft hair with its gold lights swept against Julie's flushed cheeks as she turned to stare at Bert. The huge brown eyes had no gold lights now; they looked almost black with anger. "Just what do you mean by that?" she asked dangerously.

Bert took his time passing a car, got back into his own lane. "I think your aunt is after the insurance," he said tersely. "Now before you blow your top, let me repeat

that her firm is generally considered to be on the verge
of bankruptcy. Maybe she tried to borrow money and
couldn't get it because her credit rating isn't what it
was. Maybe she had to raise cash in a hurry and this
seemed to be the best way. Fake a jewel theft and
collect the insurance."

"But that would be dishonest!"

Bert gave a short laugh. "I wouldn't exchange you for
all the gold at Fort Knox, if that's where the gold still is.
Well, dishonesty has been known to occur."

"Not to Aunt Georgia! Never!" Small fists clenched
in her lap.

"Look, honey," Bert said earnestly, ignoring her furious anger, "your aunt can cheat an insurance company if
she wants to. That doesn't concern me unless it concerns
you. But I don't want you involved in anything off-color.
Get out of there. If you won't marry me, then look for a
job. Somewhere. Anywhere. But get out before you are
tangled up with these monkeyshines."

The big Lincoln moved noiselessly down Park Avenue, its speed dropping to twenty miles, to ten, stopping
for lights, creeping in bumper-to-bumper traffic. As they
came closer to Grand Central, there were fewer apartment buildings and more towering glass and steel office
buildings. The car pulled in at the curb where a narrow
dark stone house stubbornly held its ground between
two huge apartment buildings.

Julie opened the door before Bert could move. "I can
handle my suitcase," she said crisply. "You don't need to
get out."

He turned to look at her, forcing the furious girl to
meet his steady, loving eyes. He put a hand over hers.
"You don't need me or you don't want me?"

"Don't want you," she retorted. "Not until you can
apologize for what you think about Aunt Georgia. She
has been a mother and a friend and a companion, all in
one. And aside from that, she couldn't be dishonest. It
isn't in her. She just couldn't."

"All right." He withdrew his hand. "I probably
wouldn't love you so much if you weren't as staunch as
steel. But you aren't stupid, Julie, and you're as honest
as you are loyal. Keep your eyes open. Doesn't it strike

you as funny that this burglary was staged when you were away? At least I can say this for your aunt; she didn't want to involve you if she could help it."

"Oh!" she exclaimed in exasperation over his incomprehensible stubbornness.

"Shall I take your suitcase?" asked the narrow-faced butler.

"Thank you, Perkins. In my room, please. Is the Princess at home?"

"Her Highness is in the library. A business appointment."

Bert leaned over as Julie slipped out of the car. "I'll keep on turning up," he told her, "because you've become a habit with me. One of those bad habits that are hard to break, like biting your nails." He grinned at her and her anger melted. It wasn't possible to stay angry with anyone as sweet-tempered as Bert. "I'll take the car around to your aunt's garage. Good-bye for now, honey." He waved a cheerful hand and the Lincoln slid away from the curb.

II

For a moment Julie watched as the Lincoln moved into the lane of cars. She was always heartsore when she parted with Bert in anger, but then, somehow, it happened again and again. Realizing that Perkins was holding the front door open for her, she crossed the sidewalk quickly and entered the house that had been home most of her life.

Like many old New York houses, it was narrow, one room wide, with a staircase at the right, a tessellated marble floor, a chandelier which the Princess had brought back from the Florentine palace after the death of her husband, and which was always lighted to counteract the dimness of the ground floor.

At the left there was a long drawing room with floor-length windows on the front, with dramatic gold draperies that not only counteracted the lack of sunshine by day, but by night were drawn to shut out curious eyes of passersby and the endless rumble of traffic on Park Avenue.

The dining room at the back was bright, opening on one of those unexpected hidden gardens that occur so often in the heart of New York City where it seems that no growing thing could possibly thrive, but where a small patch of lawn and a cutting garden and one tree managed to survive, although with more care and expense than was expended on the big garden of prize-winning roses in Westchester.

The middle room was a windowless library, the walls book-lined except the one facing the hall door where there was a fireplace over which hung a portrait of Dino Sobelli, so cleverly lighted that the eyes seemed to be alive, the mouth about to smile. He had been a singularly

10

handsome man. No wonder, Julie often thought when she stared at the portrait, her aunt had never really recovered from his death. No wonder she had kept so busy that there was no time for a private life. No wonder she had never displayed any interest in the men who had asked her to marry them, even the old and devoted friend, Brooks Mansfield, who took her to dinner and theaters, escorted her wherever she wished to go, always faithful, always hoping that someday she would turn to him, that eventually she would grow weary of the life of a solitary woman and would need more than a business, however thriving it might be, to fill her mind and her heart.

As a rule the library door was left open but now it was closed, and Julie remembered that the butler had said her aunt was engaged with some business appointment. Normally the Princess refused to discuss business at home. Perhaps this was some investigator inquiring about the theft of her jewelry.

Perkins had carried her suitcase to the small elevator that had been built in beside the dining room at the back of the hallway. It was just large enough for three people, providing none of them was very big. She shook her head at the butler, who pushed the button and the door closed behind him.

Julie started quietly up the carpeted stairs. She had nearly reached the landing when she heard a man say, "You aren't losing your nerve, are you?" She had never heard the voice before, a deep quiet voice.

"I'm scared half out of my wits." That was Aunt Georgia's soft contralto, the voice that was so effective on the rare occasions when she was persuaded to make speeches or television appearances.

"Have you changed your mind?"

"It's a bit late for that, isn't it? After these months of planning. After taking the major step."

"Not if you don't want to go ahead. I've never liked the idea of having a woman involved in this, in spite of the fact that I'm responsible for it. But, in the circumstances, you seemed to be a natural."

"I told you that I would go through with it. I intend to do so." Aunt Georgia had never sounded like that before. Julie did not mean to eavesdrop, she was not even aware that she was doing so. All she was sure of was that something was terribly wrong.

"If you are absolutely sure—"

"I am sure," Aunt Georgia said.

"At least you know what you're up against. That is, you know as much as the rest of us do. It's a dangerous game."

"I am prepared for that."

The man with the voice like a low-toned bell laughed softly. "More power to you. Just don't give away your hand. You're apt to be rather trusting, aren't you?"

"I don't have that reputation," the Princess said dryly. "Actually, I am regarded as hardheaded, but it's true I am not as close-mouthed as you."

"I?" The man sounded surprised.

"I've know you—how long, Mark? Four months? And you still manage to remain a mystery man though you know more about me now than anyone on earth has ever learned or guessed. Don't you have any human weaknesses?"

"Plenty of them." He seemed amused. "But I don't share your particular weakness for confiding in people. That's easy for me, of course. I'm not married."

"Why aren't you? As you are nearly twenty years younger than I, it's all right for me to tell you that you are a singularly attractive man. I imagine other women have not failed to tell you so."

"Once bitten twice shy," Mark said. "Anyhow, I've had no time for love. Well, Princess, we go ahead then, according to plan."

"According to plan," she agreed. "There's a quotation that has been haunting me all morning, something about 'And let the heavens fall.'"

"As they well may," he said coolly. "It's always as well to be prepared for the worst. This situation is like a time fuse. The trouble is that we have no way of knowing when it will be lighted. You've been warned about that, of course. Remember, you are not to get in touch with me. Whether you notice it or not—and I hope you won't—I'll be keeping an eye on you. Or someone like me will be keeping an eye on you." Was there a threat implied in the words?

They were at the library door now, and Julie realized that she had been deliberately listening to a private conversation. Very private. She ran up the stairs, past the magnificent suite on the second floor that was the domain of her aunt and that was so frequently photographed in magazines of design and home decoration, on up a narrower flight to her room on the third floor. It was on the front of the house, and she skirted the suitcase Perkins had set down, ran to the window, flung it open, leaned out.

A man emerged from the house, ignored a taxi that had drawn up hopefully, and began to walk south toward Grand Central Station. A tall man with broad shoulders and a slim build, no hat on thick dark hair. He walked with the confidence of a man who knows where he is going and has the assurance that nothing can stop him.

A nursemaid, clutching by one hand a small child who was just learning to walk, and a dog's leash held in the other, was strolling toward him. The dog ran around the child, entangling him in the leash, and the small uncertain legs collapsed as the youngster sat down hard on the sidewalk.

The dark-haired man stopped short, bent to extricate the plump body, swung him high over his head as he started to cry, made him laugh, and set him firmly on his feet. For the first time Julie saw his face. He had deep-set eyes, a good nose, and sensitively curved lips counteracted by an aggressive chin. Unquestionably an attractive man now that his grim face was lighted by a tender amusement as he returned the child to his nurse. He nodded in acknowledgment of the nurse's thanks, and continued on his way.

Not until he had become lost in the crowds thronging all approaches to Grand Central did Julie realize that she was still hanging out of the window, a thing she had been taught not to do before she was ten years old. She straightened up, noticed the film of soot on her dress from the windowsill, and brushed it away with an impatient hand. Of all the ridiculous things! What had possessed her? She had followed that deep beautiful voice as the children of Hamelin had once followed the Pied Piper.

ii

When lunch was announced, Julie found only one place had been set at the table in the sunny dining room. Her Highness had a luncheon engagement and a number of business appointments, but she would be home for dinner and hoped Miss Bryce would be free. There was something important she wanted to discuss with her. That, of course, Julie thought, would be the jewel robbery of the night before.

While Wheelock, the pretty young waitress, removed the vichyssoise and served a salmon soufflé, fresh asparagus hollandaise, tiny hot rolls, and poured hot coffee over ice in a long glass, Julie asked her about the robbery.

"No one knows how he could have got in, miss. Her Highness had gone out for dinner. Luckily she was wearing her favorite diamond bracelet. Then when she came home and Simone was helping her undress, she sent her out of the room for a minute. I suppose she meant to put the bracelet in her safe. But who would ever have dreamed there was a safe built right into the bed? So, well, then she screamed and Simone came running in, thinking she had fallen, and there was a kind of metal drawer all lined with velvet in the side of the bed, standing wide open, Simone says. Or perhaps you have seen it, miss."

Julie shook her head. "No, I've never seen it. I just knew it was there."

"Well, it was empty. The robbery must have taken place sometime after the Princess left for dinner, just about eight that was, and before she got home at eleven. But this house—locked up like a vault! You know how careful Perkins always is. And the way they questioned us servants as though we didn't have feelings like other people—"

"That's their job," Julie said soothingly. "There was

nothing personal in it, and I know how much my aunt trusts all of you." Her ready sympathy, the warmth in her voice, the friendliness of her manner, helped ease the maid's resentment.

"Well, I guess—anyhow, none of us got much sleep, I can tell you. Pictures and fingerprints and what-were-you-doing and looking here and poking there. Searched everything in my room, even the dresser drawers."

"Perhaps something can be arranged to get you a day off this week," Julie said, fearing that her aunt was in danger of losing her well-trained staff.

"That would be swell! My boyfriend has Thursdays and we've been hoping we might spend a day at Coney Island and maybe go swimming while it's so hot."

"I'll see what I can do."

"That's like you, miss. Thank you very much."

That afternoon seemed endless to Julie. In spite of her fierce defense of her aunt to Bert Wilson she found it difficult, now that she was on the spot, to believe in the jewel robbery. Was it possible that her aunt had embarked on some scheme to defraud her insurance company? Julie could not accept that. Her aunt had taught her to value honesty more than any other quality. Not only honesty in dealing with others but with herself.

"Never lie to yourself," she had told her niece over and over. "It's so desperately easy. We try to make ourselves look better to ourselves than we are. We gloss over our own selfish and unkind motives. When you find yourself doing that, be as tough on that girl Julie as you would be on anyone else you caught being dishonest."

No, Aunt Georgia could not be taking part in a crooked scheme. But what was the truth about the jewel robbery? Had the jewels really been stolen? Had Aunt Georgia secretly sold them for cash? Was she pretending they had been stolen in order to collect the insurance? Those were the only possibilities that Julie could imagine.

But even if one were to assume the worst, that Princess Sobelli was deliberately staging a fake jewel theft, she was a hardheaded and realistic businesswoman. She would know that an intensive investigation would be made of theft on so large a scale, a quarter of a million dollars' worth of jewelry. She would know that no amateur job could possibly deceive trained men. It was too terribly dangerous. To be caught attempting such a swindle would not only ruin the Sobelli business but the Princess's reputation; it might, Julie supposed, even mean a prison sentence. She had no idea what the law might be in regard to insurance fraud.

"It is a dangerous game," the man called Mark had said, and Aunt Georgia had replied, "I am prepared for that." Then she had said something about those months of planning and having taken the major step.

As there were few of her friends in the city during the hot season, Julie had no engagement to fill up the afternoon. The wardrobe which her aunt provided was so extensive there was no excuse for shopping, and anyhow she had no desire to go into the scorching breathless street and leave the comfortable air-conditioned house.

She drifted down to the library where she picked up a book, turned the pages idly, looking at the two big chairs drawn close together where her aunt and the man Mark had talked of danger. Very attractive, Aunt Georgia had said. Not married. He didn't seem to have much use for women. He could keep secrets, he said, because he had no wife. Once bitten twice shy. No time for love.

It was a relief when the long afternoon had dragged to an end and the time came to dress for dinner. From her own room Julie heard her aunt's voice as she spoke to Perkins and walked swiftly up the stairs. As a rule she didn't use the elevator because she wanted to keep in shape. In her position she could not afford to have heavy hips and a sprawling figure, she said, though she had small occasion for worry, as she still retained the lithe body of a girl. Julie did not go down to her rooms on the second floor, knowing that after a busy day her aunt liked to be undisturbed while her maid brushed her hair and she spent a long time in a scented bath and creamed her face and performed all the beauty rites which had made her famous and wealthy.

When Julie had slipped into a sleeveless silk sheath of brown with gold flecks in it that matched her eyes and the tints of her hair, the Princess's maid, Simone, tapped at the door.

"Her Highness wondered whether you needed any help."

"Oh, thank you, Simone. You can zip me up."

While the maid fastened her dress, Julie looked at her in the mirror. Like the waitress's, her eyes were shadowed from lack of sleep and her mouth twitched nervously. She seemed to be on the brink of tears.

"What is it, Simone?" Julie asked gently.

The girl started at the unexpected sound of her voice. "Have you heard about the robbery, miss?"

"It was on the radio when I was driving in this morning and I asked about it at lunch. Wheelock said you'd all been having a most unpleasant time. I'm so sorry you had to be bothered."

"Oh, miss," Simone said, her accent more in evidence because she was upset, "I think the *gendarmes*—the police—suspect me. I am Her Highness's personal maid. They are sure I knew about the safe. They—"

"The Princess knows how reliable you are, Simone, and how trustworthy. She would never let anything happen to you. Never."

There was a fleeting look of disbelief in the girl's face. "Not everyone is as kind as you, miss." Seeing that Julie was annoyed by the implied criticism of her aunt, she added, her voice expressionless, "You will find Her Highness in the drawing room."

Julie nodded and ran down the stairs to the second floor, went more slowly, sedately, down the broader flight to the main floor. Usually eager to see her aunt and to pour out the news, she felt oddly hesitant tonight.

Georgia Sobelli was seated in a great carved chair in the drawing room. She had the kind of beauty that, Julie was well aware, she herself could never achieve. Her features were nearly perfect—her profile was a cameo, her coal-black hair which she proudly refused to tint had wings of white over the ears. She was well aware of their dramatic effect. With her big black eyes and her magnolia skin the effect was startling. Tonight she wore a long dress of white and, because she either mocked at fashion or created her own, accepting whatever seemed attractive and becoming from every period, she held a fan of black ostrich plumes. What would have seemed theatrical on anyone else was simply a frame for her personality when worn by Princess Sobelli.

She was opening and closing the fan in one lovely hand but her eyes stared into space. Julie had to speak twice before she turned with a nervous start.

"Hello, darling," she said gaily. "How do you manage to look as crisp and fresh as a daffodil in this ghastly heat? It was nearly ninety today and the air-conditioning failed on the executive floor. I finally had to close the office and send the staff home before the girls started fainting. Fortunately the shop was all right. How was the weekend? Did you hear from the Jacobsons? They meant to call you. They are leaving for Europe tonight and they wanted to say goodbye."

It was not like Aunt Georgia to rush into feverish speech. "Did Bert drive down with you? Such a nice lad, isn't he, and so devoted. Quite a Galahad except, of course, for the red hair. You don't think of Galahad with red hair, somehow. You remember that famous and sentimental picture of Galahad? One of my great disillusionments as a child was learning that a woman had posed for it."

For a moment the Princess paused and Julie broke into nervous laughter. "What's the matter with you, tearing on that way? I never knew you to do it before."

"Oh, just—nothing. I've—missed you, I suppose."

That wasn't like Aunt Georgia either. She had been a loving and devoted aunt, almost a mother, but she was a woman who rarely expressed her affection in words.

"I wish to goodness," Julie told her fervently, "I could have been here with you last night. When I think of that happening—"

"Last night?" For a moment the Princess's eyes looked blank. "Oh, you mean the robbery. My dear child, my one consolation is that you were not here. Such a nuisance! Everyone in the house was kept up almost all night. It's a wonder to me I still have a staff."

"Can't you give each of them a special day to make up for it? And tell them how sorry you are they got involved through no fault of their own? They would appreciate that even more than the holiday."

There was a curious smile on the Princess's lips. "What a nice child you are! I suppose everyone in the house has already confided in you. Yes, I'll talk to them."

"How do you suppose the burglar got in?"

One beautiful hand, the diamond bracelet her husband had given her clasped around a slender wrist, was raised in protest. "Please, darling, not a word. Half the night there were police in the house prowling around. It will be no surprise if I lose my whole staff, the way the poor things were questioned and badgered and searched. And today the insurance company descended on me. I don't think I could bear to say one more word about that wretched burglary tonight."

"But, Aunt Georgia, I just wondered—"

"I mean it, Julie. I've had all I can bear." The usually controlled voice was edged with sharpness, with impatience.

"I only—there's nothing wrong, is there? Surely you can tell me that much."

"Wrong?" The black fan swirled open, snapped shut. "What on earth do you mean?"

"That man who was here this morning, the one you called Mark. I heard—"

"What!" The word came out like an explosion.

"Oh, nothing. I just wondered—it sounded as though there might be some trouble."

"Oh, that was the insurance investigator. Of course there is bound to be some trouble, filling out forms and all that sort of boredom. Tiresome, but nothing to worry about. Now, please, please, Julie, give me a little rest from all that unpleasantness."

Julie's heart sank. She swallowed hard. "Of course, Aunt Georgia. Not another word."

"Your Highness is served."' Perkins spoke from the doorway. The Princess got up swiftly, as though she were escaping from something, and led the way to the dining room.

Usually, even after the shortest absence, Julie was bubbling over with news, but tonight the restraint imposed on her by the Princess made it difficult for her to speak. The questions that crowded their way to her lips must not be spoken, for some reason. Something was terribly wrong and she was not allowed to help. At least, as Bert had said, her aunt did not intend to involve her.

Halfway through dinner the Princess began to talk. "Do you have many plans for the summer, Julie; plans you couldn't or wouldn't want to change?"

Julie looked up in surprise. "Nearly everyone I know is out of town. I've had some invitations, of course: the Hamiltons have asked me to go on their cruise, and I've been asked to take part in the tennis tournament at the country club. But I'd rather stay with you."

"Always hoping that some day I'll put you to work?" The Princess laughed. "No, Julie, you aren't a business-woman. One of these days, and probably sooner than later, you will marry, and you simply are not a woman to divide your interests. All or nothing, if I know any-thing about you. Before long, of course, I'll have to start training someone to assist me and eventually to replace me but it won't be you. That's not the life I see ahead for you."

"But suppose you marry again," Julie said, half laugh-ing. "You're an all-or-nothing person, too."

Her aunt looked at her with shadowed eyes. "I will never marry again. For me Dino was the once-in-a-lifetime man."

"Aunt Georgia," Julie began impulsively, "please don't think I am impertinent. I don't mean to be."

"You couldn't be, my dear. What is it?"

Julie waited while Wheelock removed dishes, brought the next course, returned to the kitchen. "I was thinking, perhaps," she said when they were alone, "that—well, after all, the Prince died a long time ago and you're still so lovely. It's such a—waste."

"You are very sweet, Julie, but Dino's death—"

"Can't you start over?"

Her aunt's face hardened unexpectedly. "No. There is too much—unfinished business."

"I don't understand," said Julie, looking at her aunt's face, which was suddenly that of a stranger.

"I didn't mean you to." The Princess nibbled at a mint. She went on briskly, "I've been thinking, Julie, that if you really want to help me with the business—"

"Oh, I do! I do!"

"I'd like to send you abroad. Right away, if it won't interfere with your summer plans or spoil things for you. I'm preparing some big surprises for the Christmas trade. Sobelli, Inc., is going to sweep the field: exquisite perfume bottles I'm having designed in Florence, some fascinating ceramic compacts made in England, a new perfume that my chemist in Paris is creating. What with one thing and another, I can't leave New York now. Do you suppose you could act as my deputy? Check to see how things are progressing and report to me?"

"I'd love it!" Julie exclaimed. In her excitement she forgot all about the burglary.

III

In the next two weeks Julie was completely absorbed in the multitude of problems associated with planning the trip, renewing her passport, being vaccinated, acquiring new luggage, and making a careful list of the people whom she was to interview and of the tasks she was to perform in Europe. Not until she was at the airport, prepared to board a jet for Italy, did she have leisure to remember the disappearance of her aunt's jewelry. To her great surprise, the story had disappeared completely out of the news. If any official inquiries were still being made, she did not hear of them.

Bert had managed to get a few hours of leave and he came to see her off, red hair sticking up wildly on his head, his eyes sober for once.

"How long will you be gone?" he asked her.

"I don't know. Probably a month. Maybe six weeks."

"Well, you shouldn't forget me in that length of time." He looked at the orchid pinned to her shoulder. "Which of your admirers gave you that?"

She laughed. "Not one of my admirers, one of Aunt Georgia's. This came from Brooks Mansfield."

"Two guys in the same boat," Bert said, grinning. "He's as faithful to your aunt as I am to you." He gave her a newspaper clipping. "Something to read on the plane. It's especially interesting if you read between the lines." He leaned forward, kissed her inexpertly, the kiss falling on the side of her small nose.

From her seat by the window she looked down, a long way down, and saw Bert's flaming red hair, as he stood smiling up at her. Behind him there was a man who had just turned away, a man with black hair and broad shoulders who moved like a soldier. Her face lit up with a smile so radiant that it transformed her. And then she realized that the man was not making the flight. Apparently, like Bert, he had come to see someone off.

Julie was surprised at the wave of disappointment that swept over her. Before the plane was airborne she had forgotten Bert's clumsy farewell kiss but she remembered the black-haired man. She unfastened her seat belt, tucked her handbag beside her, and remembered the clipping she still clutched in her hand. It was from the magazine section of a Sunday paper. Bert had marked the article with a blue pencil:

SMUGGLING NOW BIG BUSINESS

After providing a minor headache for the government for over a hundred years, smuggling has now entered the major league and became big business, involving everything from jewelry and drugs to secret designs for armaments. Almost no legitimate industry is completely free of the threat of smugglers.

A field that was once controlled by petty gangsters has come into the hands not only of major criminals but of people who stand high in the economic, social, and political life of the country. It is this vast network—

That was all there was. Julie read it, half puzzled, turned the paper over to see whether she was reading the wrong story, but the one on the other side had to deal with the protection of wildlife in Africa. Read between the lines, Bert had told her. She read the clipping again. Smuggling? What was it that Bert was trying to tell her or to hint to her?

She gave up the puzzle. There would be plenty of time to ask him about it when she got back. Meantime, a magic world stretched out before her: Florence, Rome, Paris, London. It couldn't possibly be as wonderful as her expectations, she warned herself. She was bound to be disappointed.

But she was to remember that trip all her life because it was so much more wonderful than her dreams. Her aunt must have spent many hours arranging every detail, from her arrival in Italy by plane to her departure by ship in England to return to New York.

Wherever she went there were escorts to take her to dinner and to dance, assistants from the Sobelli firm to show her the new designs and detail the progress of their new products; there were managers of each branch to show her the operation of the exotic beauty parlors that were an adjunct to the main business, the manufacturing of cosmetics. The shops themselves, as the world's most luxurious beauty salons, helped women to make the best of themselves and to retain a reasonable semblance of youth well into middle age.

"Perhaps," the head of the Paris office told her with a smile, "we have discovered little that is new since Cleopatra cast her spell over Mark Antony, but we send women out of here more confident than when they came in."

Julie laughed. "Even when they aren't really prettier?"

"It isn't what they are, it's what they think they are. For instance, a woman who believes she is loved is more beautiful than a woman who lacks that assurance. We are purveyors of the dream, Miss Julie."

He chuckled reminiscently. "Not always, of course. I remember one time a woman came here and had everything we could do for her: her hair was shaped and tinted and given a permanent wave—a completely new hairdo. She had a facial massage and a trained makeup woman worked on her face. She had a manicure and a pedicure, and all the rest." He chuckled again. "I must say that it cost her a small fortune. But to her it was well worth it: she had been transformed. She was simply radiant and self-confident when she was ready to leave. Then it happened that she turned to our receptionist. 'Well,' she demanded expectantly, 'what do you think of me?' And the receptionist looked at her, smiled in sympathy for her predicament, and said, 'I am so sorry, madam. We haven't time to do a thing for you today.'" He burst into explosive laughter and Julie joined him.

During the hectic days of the trip, Julie stopped religiously every night before she went to bed, however late it might be, to tick off the items she had accomplished for her aunt.

There was only one thing she had done on her own,

without an escort. She had been impelled, perhaps by Bert's questions about her aunt's inexplicable neglect, to visit the old Sobelli palace. Her aunt had loved her dead husband; she had spent great sums in furnishing the Park Avenue house and the sprawling country place in Westchester. Why was she letting the Sobelli palace crumble in ruins?

The large edifice was impressive from the outside but it was unoccupied, except for a caretaker, who seemed astonished at having the Princess's niece visit the place, and obviously horrified for fear she planned to stay there. He made no attempt to conceal his consternation and dismay.

"No cook," he told her with wide gestures to accentuate the words. "No maids. Nothing."

Nothing, indeed. The marble floor struck a chill through her bones, though the day was hot. The immense building had long been shut up. Moving from room to room, Julie noticed spots of dampness on the ceilings, saw that tapestries were moth-eaten and so dusty that she sneezed if she stirred them; most of the furniture had been removed.

The caretaker shambled after her reluctantly, opening shutters, wiping off a chair now and then so she could sit down, throwing wide a window with which he had to struggle because it had swollen tight.

In answer to her friendly questions he told her that he had been a kitchen boy in the days of Prince Sobelli. Such a handsome man. Always laughing. Then the illness and the pain. Then the money dwindled away. And all of a sudden he had died.

"How long has it been since anyone has been here?" Julie asked, trying to peer through windows almost obscured by cobwebs.

The caretaker hesitated. "Since the Princess left the palace many years ago, no one has—lived here."

"But someone has come to visit?" Looking around her Julie found it incredible that anyone would stay in the place overnight.

"To visit? No, I don't think so."

"Don't *think* so?"

"It's sounds and footsteps and lights, though there is

no electricity here now. As though there was someone in the next room. No, I don't go around the palace, me, if I can help it." The man's manner was half sheepish, half defiant, but he was genuinely frightened. What a caretaker he was! Scared of his own shadow. Julie wondered what would happen if she suddenly turned on him and shouted, "Boo!" He would probably faint. She stifled a giggle.

Nonetheless, to her annoyance, it began to seem that she heard soft footsteps ahead of her. She had an impression that a door closed just as she looked at it. All nerves, of course. Unbridled imagination. Because the timorous caretaker imagined things, she had begun to do so.

In one of the huge bedrooms she idly tried a door; it refused to open. The closets were all locked, the caretaker explained. They probably held some old belongings of the Prince. He did not have any keys. The Princess might have them. He knew nothing about it.

It was a relief to leave the palace at last, with its stale cold air, and a chill, she thought, like a mausoleum. In fact, the whole palace was like a mausoleum. A fortune would be required to repair it and make it habitable. Habitable? No one would want to live there. Beautiful as the rooms were, they were ghost-ridden. Even Aunt Georgia would find it impossible to recall her happy days with Dino in this empty shell of a building. No wonder she had abandoned it. To attempt adequate repairs would simply be to throw good money after bad.

Julie had gone alone to the palace from her hotel because she did not want any of her aunt's business associates or social acquaintances to know that she had been there. She herself did not know why she felt it important to keep her visit a secret. She knew only that she must come.

When she left the palace, ushered out by the greatly relieved Giuseppe, she looked around, uncertain of her way, not knowing where to get a taxi, and not sure how to get back to her hotel. A slim man with fair hair had paused near the entrance to light a cigarette. He was unmistakably American. After a moment's hesitation Julie asked him how to get back to her hotel, repeated the directions he gave her to make sure she had them right, and thanked him.

He looked her over with open curiosity, obviously wondering why she had been in the deserted palace. He smiled at her. "Sure you can find your hotel? I'm not busy."

She laughed, refused his offer to accompany her, and set off briskly. Behind her she heard a man's footsteps and she was aware that the man was following her. She wasn't afraid. No reason to be afraid on the streets of Florence in broad daylight. Nonetheless she found herself hastening. She was relieved when she caught sight of her hotel. How absurd she was! Just a man following a pretty girl. But it had not seemed like that. There had been something disturbing, something evil about that encounter.

It wasn't until she had reached her hotel that she knew what had been puzzling her. Heavy on the stale air of the palace rooms had hung a haze of cigarette smoke, the scent of Turkish tobacco. The fair-haired American who had been outside the palace, directed her to her hotel, and then followed her, had been lighting a Turkish cigarette.

That night as usual she sent an airmail note to her aunt, describing the city, the shop and office, and telling her about the pleasantness of her escort. She did not mention her visit to the palace. It would, she told herself, only arouse unhappy memories in her aunt. As a result, she did not mention her fleeting encounter with the American. It did not seem important at the time.

ii

Not until the first week in September did Julie leave England by ship. "Why fly back," her aunt had written, "when you can have a nice, leisurely voyage?"

Apparently Princess Sobelli was not anxious for her niece's return; indeed, she seemed more than willing to have her extend the European visit as long as possible. And not once in the weeks of her absence was there any reference to the jewel theft.

Julie was seated at the Captain's table, and the young officer who was second in command, an engaging man whose features were enhanced by his smart uniform, seemed to be dazzled by her. Although his position required that he relieve the Captain of as many of his social obligations as possible, he had eyes for no one but the pretty girl with the rose-petal complexion and the huge brown eyes.

With one exception, all the passengers at the Captain's table were middle-aged or elderly couples who took the infatuation of the young officer and his absorption in the lovely girl in good part. The exception was a woman of thirty who was exquisitely groomed and so beautifully dressed that she gave an illusion of being better looking than she was. Her chief attraction was her vivacity, which lighted up a narrow face and made it interesting. She was constantly in motion, making quick nervous gestures with hands that glittered with diamonds. She was introduced as Lady Maydock. Perhaps because of the young officer's interest in Julie, Lady Maydock ignored her for the first couple of days beyond a distant "Good morning" or "Good evening."

It was not until the third day out that Julie saw the man called Mark. She had been lying in her deck chair, an unopened book on her lap, looking at the rise and fall of the horizon, dimly aware of the passengers near her talking with the easy friendship of shipboard acquaintances. A man in slacks and sweater walked past her chair briskly. Something about the confident walk, the broad shoulders, the glossy black hair was familiar. Julie's eyes opened wide and she sat up, watching him stride along the deck and out of sight. A moment later the young officer came to perch on the footrest of her chair. As she had already become familiar with the symptoms of a young man about to declare his eternal devotion, she tried hastily to sidetrack him. She despised girls who took pride in collecting scalps and encouraging men whom they had no intention of marrying.

"Tell me," she asked, "why did you pick this career?"

"I've always been crazy about the sea," he told her. "I'm never really happy when I am so far away that I can't hear the sound of the surf. Cities stifle me." He gestured, laughing, toward the limitless horizon. "I need a lot of elbowroom."

Seeing that she was genuinely interested, he told her about starting on a merchant ship. In a way he had preferred it to a passenger vessel because the work was more varied and interesting. But it got to be too much for him. On his last three voyages the government boys had searched the ship and the cargo and the crew.

"I don't believe anything bigger than a pin escaped them."

"Why?"

"Smuggling," he told her briefly. "Especially dope. You wouldn't believe the number of ways people can think of to smuggle dope. The men who were doing the searching found dope in canned fish, in packaged cheese, in innocent-looking letters in men's pockets, in the cuffs of their trousers and the seams of their jackets. Close one door and a dozen others are opened by smugglers. And the worst of it was that some of them were people of high reputation, who got involved almost by accident, or who were blackmailed into it, or who looked for easy money because their businesses were failing. It got to be too much for me. I hated the whole thing."

Seeing his grim expression Julie asked in surprise, "But why did it disturb you so terribly? After all, you weren't to blame for the dope traffic."

"I have a kid brother who shot heroin in college just for the experience. And he got hooked. He went through hell before he was cured. I would like to see all dope smugglers sent up for life. They are worse than murderers. Anyhow, I quit the merchant service and got a job on a passenger ship."

For the first time since she had left New York Julie remembered the torn fragment of a clipping given her by Bert. He had said it was interesting if she read between the lines. Smuggling had become big business. All kinds of people were involved, even some who had high social, economic, and political positions. Smuggling. What had Bert tried to tell her?

"And then," the young officer said, leaning forward earnestly, "it paid off, changing from merchant to passenger ships. Because I met you."

Julie tried to distract his attention, to forestall a proposal. "Who are they?"

He turned to where a man and woman stood together at the rail. They appeared to be looking out to sea but they were talking quickly in low tones. There was an unmistakable air of familiarity about them as though they had talked this way many times before.

"The woman is Lady Maydock. You must have met her because she sits at the Captain's right. The one with all the diamonds. The man—" For the first time the loquacious Officer hesitated. His manner was more reserved when he said, "His name is Mark Sefton. We've had him with us on several trips."

"I suppose his job takes him abroad a lot," Julie said. "I think someone mentioned that he is an insurance investigator."

"Not Sefton," the officer said, sounding like a man who is sure of his facts.

As though aware that he was being discussed Mark Sefton turned his head and looked directly at Julie. She sustained the scrutiny of those brilliant eyes for a moment, feeling that she was being X-rayed, and then her lashes dropped, her cheeks burned.

The officer sprang to his feet as Lady Maydock came up to the deck chair, followed by the black-haired man.

"Miss Bryce," she exclaimed, "I've just realized who you are! A niece of Princess Sobelli. My dear, she is one of my most valued friends. And do let me present a fellow passenger who so wants to meet you. Mark Sefton. Miss Bryce."

"How do you do?" Julie said coldly, annoyed because she had allowed the man's searching look to disturb her.

"How do you do?" he said in the deep voice that had so stirred her when she first heard it. Recalling how she had leaned out of a window to watch him walk up the street, Julie, to her furious embarrassment, felt herself blushing again. A disturbing man, this Mark Sefton. And if he really wanted to know her, there was no trace of it in his remote politeness.

The officer nodded to Julie and went regretfully away. Lady Maydock hesitated and then moved off with a friendly wave of the hand.

Mark Sefton looked at the footrest as though he would like to sit there. Then he said, "There will be dancing tonight. I hope you'll dance with me, Miss Bryce?"

"Thank you. I'd like to."

When he had gone she lay back in her deck chair, staring out at the gray ocean. The officer must have been wrong. Her aunt would not have lied to her. But if Mark Sefton was not an insurance investigator, what was he?

IV

It was not until she was dressing for dinner that Julie discovered that her cabin had been searched. Nothing was upset but nothing was quite in the order in which she kept it. Handkerchiefs were on top of her gloves instead of underneath. Her stockings, usually arranged according to shade, were mixed up. A coat had been taken down and rehung with one shoulder sagging off the hanger.

Nothing had been taken. Such simple jewelry as she wore was still in its box. A feverish check revealed that nothing was gone from her handbag. Her billfold was untouched; her passport was safe; her traveler's checks had moved mysteriously from the zippered compartment where she usually kept them, and her little address book was in the place they normally occupied. Small things, but she was sure that her belongings had been carefully and minutely searched.

Only when she was ready for her cosmetics did she become aware of the extent of that inexplicable search. Someone had stirred up her jar of cold cream. An orange stick was covered with skin lotion, indicating it had been used to prod the contents of the plastic bottle. The ends of her lipstick had been cut off. Her face powder had been disturbed and the big soft powder puff had been ripped open.

Julie's first question was not "who?" It was "why?" Nothing had been taken and yet every scrap of her belongings had been examined. Why? Why? What in heaven's name would anyone expect to find in her luggage or her clothing?

In answer to Julie's ring, a startled stewardess said that no other passenger had complained of having his cabin entered, and that perhaps Miss Bryce had forgotten the exact order in which she put things. Anyhow, as nothing had been taken, there was no real cause for complaint.

Julie let it go. Nothing, as the stewardess pointed out, had been taken. It was only her impression that someone had searched her cabin, had disturbed her clothes, had examined her cosmetics minutely. It occurred to Julie that some competitor of Princess Sobelli might have been examining her cosmetics and then she realized the absurdity of that. They were all available in stores and this hidden search was unnecessary. Perhaps, as the stewardess obviously believed, she had imagined the whole thing.

The most disturbing element of the whole mysterious business was that when she had entered her cabin she had been aware of the scent of Turkish cigarettes. As she never smoked, someone else must have done so in the cabin. She decided to let the matter rest until she could talk it over with the young officer.

It was the thought of him and his confidences about his brother that made her wonder whether someone suspected her of smuggling. That would account for the minuteness of the search. What had he told her? That the government men had not missed anything bigger than a pin. But why should she be an object of suspicion?

Meantime, she took particular trouble in preparing for the evening, selecting a soft gold dress she had bought in Paris that brought out the gold lights in her hair. She did not attempt to explain to herself why she was particularly anxious to look her best tonight. Nonetheless her heart was dancing when she went to dinner.

Lady Maydock was in black and easily the best dressed woman on shipboard. Tonight she had a gay word and a wave of her hand for Julie, who heard her explaining to the man on her right that she had just discovered Julie Bryce was the niece of her dear friend, Princess Sobelli. "You know, *the* Princess Sobelli. Cosmetics."

To Julie's disappointment the Captain occupied his own place at the table and his second in command was on duty, so she had no opportunity to talk to him about

the searching of her cabin. Later she was secretly relieved that she had had no opportunity to yield to the
temptation to confide in the officer. The more she
thought about that odd invasion of her cabin, the more
reluctant she was to discuss the incident with anyone.

After dinner there was dancing and Mark Sefton
came to claim her. At first he did not speak at all. Then
when they had danced for a few minutes he began to
ask her about her trip and she found herself telling him
about the cities she had visited, about her aunt's business, and all the stirring plans she was making for new
ways of merchandising cosmetics.

She broke off, blushing, aware that she had been
chattering as easily as she might to Bert. It never occurred to her that the information had been brought out
adroitly by a man who was exceptionally skilled at ex-
tracting information.

"Sorry, I can't expect a man to be thrilled by hearing
about cosmetics."

"I'm interested in hearing you talk about them," he
said, as he caught her eyes for an electric moment.

When the orchestra stopped for a break, he led her
over to their table. "There's a full moon tonight—come
look at it," he said, as he put her long black satin cape
over her shoulders. He caught her by the hand and they
walked out on deck. For a long time they stood leaning
on the rail, watching the path of light cut by the moon
on the water, seeing the moon itself riding high and
serene in the sky.

"It seems so—inviolate," Julie said at last. "It is odd to
think that men have landed on it, have seen a barren
landscape instead of the magic illusion we get from
here. I wish we could have kept it that way—free forever of men's muddy footsteps. I wish we had not invad-
ed the sky. I wish—" She looked up to find his eyes on
her face and he turned away at once.

"We had better go in before you're chilled," he said
abruptly, and Julie, with a pang of disappointment, left
the magic of the moonlight behind and returned to
electric lights and dance music and the sound of laughter.

"Thank you for the dance," Mark said with unexpected formality, and then he bowed and went away so quickly that she had no time for a single word, almost like a man in flight. Julie looked after him, bemused.

Behind her a woman laughed. It was Lady Maydock. "My dear," she said in amusement, "you must not let Mark Sefton sweep you off your feet."

"I—" Julie began, anger blazing in her eyes at the woman's impertinence.

Lady Maydock touched her arm. "Believe me, child, I know what I am talking about. I came very close to marrying him once. I was engaged to him and we even had the wedding plans all made. I was ready to send out invitations. And then—"

"This doesn't really concern me," Julie said hastily. She did not want to hear about it.

The older woman was smiling again, that mocking smile. "I know the symptoms. Mark isn't for you, my dear. I don't think he is for any woman. Frankly, I broke off with him because—well, for one thing he frightened me. He's a ruthless man in some ways. Anyhow, I thought it would be nicer to marry a man I could count on coming home safely. And with Mark one would never know. He doesn't have time for me in his life. Or for any woman."

No time for any woman. Julie smiled brightly at Lady Maydock, but her thoughts were in a turmoil. She made up her mind that she was going to forget Mark Sefton. Forget him now. Never let him so much as creep into her thoughts. She went down to her cabin with this determination strong in her mind. It was curious how desolate it made her feel. The man who couldn't be counted on to come home safely. The man who was not an insurance investigator. The man who frightened Lady Maydock—but had wanted to marry her! The man who had looked at Julie Bryce for one wonderful moment and then had gone away from her as quickly as he could.

Only when she had slipped into bed and turned out her light did Julie realize how odd it was that Lady Maydock had spoken of Julie's relationship to Princess

Sobelli and yet Mark had not mentioned that he too knew her aunt. It would have been the natural thing to do.

ii

Standing at the rail, Julie looked from the Statue of Liberty to the black-haired man at her side. She had seen little of Mark Sefton after the night when they had danced together. True, they ate at different tables and he rarely appeared in the lounge rooms. Occasionally he went past her on the deck. Only twice did he stop for a few casual words and then he was gone again. It became apparent that he was deliberately avoiding her.

Somewhat to Julie's surprise, Lady Maydock had devoted more and more time to her. If Julie was playing bridge, she would cut in at the first opportunity. If Julie was on deck, she would drop onto the next deck chair. And always the conversation was deftly brought around to Julie's trip, to the people she had met, the new products her aunt was preparing for the trade. Lady Maydock was as interested in all the details as Mark Sefton had been.

It was a relief to watch New York's magnificent skyline on a brilliant blue day without having Lady Maydock at her elbow, asking strange, probing questions. As she was a late riser, she was unlikely to appear until the last moment after the ship had docked.

The young officer too was busy; the night before, he had dejectedly accepted his dismissal and said goodbye. Only by chance, Julie felt, had Mark Sefton stopped beside her this morning. She had happened to see him approach, had smiled spontaneously. He had been about to pass by, he had hesitated, and then, almost reluctantly, he came to stand by her side.

"There's no sight quite like it, is there?" he commented, staring at the gleaming buildings that soared into the sky.

"Sometimes," Julie confided, "I have nightmares when I think of what bombers could do to all that beauty, to all that enormously congested mass of humanity."

"It isn't the bombers I fear," he said, "it's the rats that tunnel underground, that undermine the foundations."

He smiled unexpectedly, aware that he had struck too serious a note, and drained the gaiety from her face. "Glad to be home?" he asked lightly.

She nodded. "The trip has been fabulous. I'll never forget it. But it's good to be back." The tugs had edged the great ship toward the dock and she leaned forward, eagerly scanning the faces below, not that she really believed her aunt would be likely to meet her at such an early hour, but there was always the possibility.

Then she saw the morning sun shining on red hair, saw Bert's broad smile as he caught her attention and waved wildly. She leaned over the rail to wave at him and turned around to point him out to Mark. The latter was just moving out of sight. He had not suggested seeing her again. He had not even said good-bye.

The bleakness of that unexpected ending to the acquaintance, the finality of it, still weighed on Julie while she waited beside her luggage for the customs inspection. And at last she was on the dock and Bert was waiting patiently for her. He kissed her cheek and stood with his hands on her shoulders, looking down at her without the big smile on his face. She had never seen him so sober.

"Come on, honey. Your aunt let me borrow her car when I telephoned to say that I planned to meet you. Over this way."

As Julie paused and looked back at the ship for a moment he asked casually, "Are you looking for someone?"

"No," she assured him hastily. "Oh, no!" There was no sign of Mark Sefton. She raised her head proudly, smiled at Bert. "How grand of you to meet me."

"It's a wonder the newspaper could struggle on without me for a whole morning. No, not that way. The Lincoln's parked across the street." Something of Bert's usual zest was missing. Normally he had an endless line of nonsense but this morning he did not even ask about the trip. "Still fancy free, after seeing all the eligible men in Europe at your feet?"

She ignored the question, aware of the hot color in her cheeks. "How is Aunt Georgia?"

"I don't move in those exalted circles, lady. I called her to say I'd meet you, that's all. So far as I know, all is well. Usual hectic excitement over the Maskers Ball—it's always the most talked about social event of the season."

"What about that burglary, Bert? I haven't heard a single word about it. The whole thing just dropped out of the news."

"So I notice. Who was that black-haired guy who was standing beside you and—"

"Bert," she interrupted quickly, "what did you mean by that clipping you gave me when I left?"

"Oh, it was a vague kind of warning. Just sort of a watch-your-step sign."

"A warning to me?"

He laughed with almost his usual gaiety. "Hey, when you open your eyes that wide I'm afraid I'll fall in. Here's the car. Hope I didn't get a ticket. Nope, all is well." He helped her into the seat beside him. "How does your home town look to you, lady?"

"From this particular spot rather dusty and dirty and sordid. But on the whole—beautiful. Bert, please don't evade me. What did that clipping mean?"

For a few minutes he concentrated on getting into traffic without scratching the car. Then he said decisively, "Nope! I've given you a hint. The Lord knows I may be off the beam. I hope I am. But at least you'll be alerted. You'll be watching."

"What for?"

"Shenanigans," he told her, and he fell silent again. At last he roused himself. "Where do you want to go? House or the shop?"

"The shop," she decided, and he pulled into a space in front of a Fifth Avenue building.

A uniformed man stepped forward to open the door for her. "Welcome home, Miss Bryce."

"Thank you. Oh, Bert, thanks a lot for meeting me."

"My pleasure. I'll take your luggage home and have the car garaged. Be seeing you tonight." He waved his hand and drove away without another look at her.

The doorman went back to open the door, which had

a design in silver, the hallmark of the Sobelli Cosmetics, Inc., and Julie stepped out of the real world of Fifth Avenue into the perfume-scented dream world where women seek beauty and eternal youth.

A young woman exquisitely groomed, her hair beautifully arranged, wearing a mini skirt that was not too extreme, looked at her from behind a pretty desk that seemed to have nothing to do with anything as tiresome as business appointments. Then her face lighted in a natural smile.

"Miss Bryce! Nice to have you back."

"It's nice to be back."

"Her Highness had an early fitting at her dressmaker's but she will be here before long. Will you wait?"

Julie nodded and went past the shop where women were getting permanents, having their hair restyled, having powder mixed to blend with their complexions, having experts make them up, getting facials and manicures and all the treatments used by what the Frenchman had called "purveyors of the dream."

A small elevator with a bench upholstered in silver velvet, the walls lined with the same material so that it resembled a jewel box, took her to the executive floor where Princess Sobelli, for all the ornateness of her surroundings, conducted a hardheaded business and kept a shrewd eye on profits and the products of her competition.

Princess Sobelli, Private, read a small silver sign outside one of the doors. Julie opened it and went in. Even here the famous Sobelli perfume scented the air. The floor had silvery wall-to-wall carpeting and pale lavender brocaded draperies framed the window.

Everything about the small reception room, which doubled as a secretary's office, was elegant. Everything except for the girl herself. Drab hair of no particular color hung straight, fastened by a no-colored ribbon. There was no makeup on her face. Her light eyelashes and brows were practically invisible. Her blue linen dress was of a conservative shirtwaist type and fitted badly.

She was deeply engrossed in reading a letter. As Julie came in, she flushed, folded the letter hastily, and slid it back in its envelope. "Welcome home, Miss Bryce."

"It's nice to be home, May. How have things been here?"

"Oh," the girl said, "just about the same. Nothing really changes, you know, except for a new product now and then." There was no bitterness in her voice, only a kind of flatness.

Not for the first time Julie wondered about her aunt's faithful secretary. She was a treasure, the Princess had declared enthusiastically. Efficient, a wonderful memory, loyal, completely reliable, and trustworthy. Julie had been acquainted with May Williams for three years, more or less, and she knew nothing whatever about the girl, who remained drab and plain in an atmosphere of beauty and adornment.

"It must have been a wonderful trip," the girl said wistfully.

"Oh, it was! When do you take your vacation, May? I know you usually go after the summer rush is over."

"In October. Three weeks from now." Again there was that curious flatness in the girl's voice.

Feeling a little guilty at having so much when this girl had so little, Julie perched on the edge of the neat desk. "What are you planning to do?"

"I was—that is, I had thought of going to a resort in Vermont where I could see the changing foliage and do some horseback riding and maybe some fishing." There was a slight flush on the girl's cheeks. "Not romantic, perhaps, but it's the kind of vacation I like. That is—" Her voice dropped away.

"Has anything gone wrong?" Julie asked, with so much friendliness and sympathy in her warm voice that the secretary looked at her in surprise. "Is there anything I could do to help?"

May smiled in some amusement. "No, Miss Bryce, you couldn't possibly help. You wouldn't understand this kind of situation."

"Can't you tell me about it?"

The girl laughed rather bitterly. "Why not? I have a brother, my only living relation, in Vietnam. We've always been very close and he—well, he sees me as a more attractive person than I have ever been. Well, one of his friends over there, who has no family at all, is

coming back in October. My brother introduced us by
mail and we've been writing to each other for months,
planning the things we would do when he comes. It has
all been a lot of fun, but only make-believe. I never
thought Paul would really come, and then—"

Julie's eyes opened wide. "You mean he's—something
happened to him?"

"Oh, no. But he has been building up a picture of me
from what my brother said. And what would happen if
he really saw me as I am and tried to be polite about it?
I don't believe I could bear that." She made a defeated
gesture. "I guess I really didn't understand what ideas
he had about me until I got this letter, so now I'll have
to go away or do something drastic or make some wild
excuse so that he'll never see me."

Julie slid off the desk and stared at the drab girl, her
eyes blazing. "You—you—" she sputtered. "Of all the
ridiculous—" She broke off and tried again. "Look here,
you work for one of the most famous cosmetic compa-
nies in the world. Downstairs women are being transformed all day long. Why on earth don't you give yourself the full treatment? And what's more, I'll see that
Aunt Georgia pays for it. Your Paul is going to get the
jolt of his life."

"My Paul?" the secretary repeated.

Julie nodded emphatically. "Your Paul. If you want
him. Any woman can get any man she really wants if
she uses her head."

"You don't really believe in all those miracles, do you?
You've never had to depend on them. With your wonderful complexion and hair and your beautiful eyes
you're lovely as you are."

"You just wait," Julie said, "until Aunt Georgia gets
back."

"And what will happen then?" asked her aunt's lovely
contralto voice.

V

"Dear Julie!" The Princess pressed a soft cheek against the girl's. "How wonderful to see you. Come into my office. I don't have an appointment for an hour."

"Right away, Aunt Georgia, but first—" Rapidly Julie explained the secretary's predicament while the girl sat watching them, red with embarrassment, her hands twisting together awkwardly.

There was a moment of surprise and then, to Julie's pleasure and relief, her aunt entered into the scheme with as much interest and excitement as the girls. She brought her hands together in a quick gesture. Then she said, "Stand up."

May Williams stood and the Princess surveyed her slowly from head to foot. "Turn around. You really have a beautiful figure, if you only knew how to dress." A hand lifted the girl's hair, tilted her chin.

"Call Antoine and say I want him up here as soon as he is at leisure," she directed. "Come on, Julie. I'm eager to hear all about the trip."

She swept the girl into the big office with its windows on Fifth Avenue, with deep chairs and a fine old Florentine mirror she must have brought from her husband's palace. The room was deep-carpeted, with magnificent draperies. On the great carved desk there was a photograph in a silver frame of Prince Sobelli, and a snapshot of Julie in tennis clothes, laughing into the sun. There was nothing else but a leather engagement pad, a silver pencil, and a silver telephone.

For a moment she held Julie away from her, smiling. Then she waved her into a deep chair upholstered in silver brocade.

"I hope," Julie began, "you were satisfied with the reports I sent you."

"I was very much impressed because you were so businesslike and efficient, my dear."

"But?"

Her aunt smiled and shook her head. "But the answer is still no, my dear. You don't belong in the business world."

"Most girls earn their living."

"But I wonder how many of them would if they had any choice in the matter. Oh, I don't mean the career girls and those in professions. I mean the average girl who wants to marry and have a home and a family." The Princess was gay and smiling but she was adamant. Julie gave up with a good grace, in spite of her disappointment, and dropped the subject.

"I've been dying to know, Aunt Georgia, whatever happened about your jewelry. Was it recovered?"

A shadow crossed the beautiful, rather cold face of the Princess. "I suppose someday part of it will turn up. For the time being, let's forget it." Apparently she forgot Julie's trip too, because she did not refer to it again. "Tonight is the Maskers Ball. I suppose, as Bert met you, he told you that he is to be your escort."

"No, he just said he'd be seeing me tonight."

"I do hope that doesn't mean he was offended because I bought his ticket and sent it to him. I knew he couldn't afford to spend fifty dollars for an affair like that on his salary. I ordered an enchanting costume for you. You'll find it at home. I didn't dare hurt Bert's pride by getting him a costume but he can probably pick up something cheap or, if he prefers, simply wear a mask with his dinner clothes. Brooks Mansfield will be my escort, of course, so they are both dining at the house with us. You'll want to get home and get unpacked and rest, I suppose."

The Princess turned as Miss Williams opened the door and said, "Antoine is here."

"Antoine? Oh, yes, bring him in."

The young man who followed the secretary into the room bowed to the Princess. "Your Highness wanted to see me?"

The Princess nodded and indicated May Williams. "Look at this girl. I want you to study her, to find out what she needs: hair, skin, makeup, the works. You have—" She looked at Julie. "How long is it before this young man arrives?"

"Three weeks."

"You have three weeks to work on Miss Williams." Before her secretary could thank her, she waved an impatient hand and the girl went out, followed by the technician from the beauty parlor.

"This is going to be fun!" the Princess said to Julie. "I wish she had told me and I could have helped her long ago. Somehow I never noticed her or thought of her as a woman, just as a fine secretary. People always confide in you, don't they? Now run along, my dear. I have a busy day ahead. I'll see you tonight."

ii

The costume which the Princess had selected for Julie was that of a Spanish dancer, made of scarlet and black. When she had piled her hair on her head and topped it by a high glittering comb and picked up the exquisitely carved fan that completed the costume, Julie tried on the small black mask and laughed at the colorful figure that faced her in the mirror.

By the time she went downstairs her aunt was already waiting for her with the two devoted escorts. The Princess had selected a costume based on one in which the Tudor Queen Elizabeth had been painted, with its immense hoopskirt and its glittering jewels, though for the first time since Julie could remember, the jewels, which were an essential part of the costume, were fakes, except for the diamond bracelet.

Bert Wilson had solved the problem of a costume by turning a bedspread into the toga of a Roman emperor, but the impersonation was not very effective because of his red hair and thin figure. Brooks Mansfield, who had been Georgia Sobelli's devoted escort for ten years, was most uncomfortably arrayed in a suit of tin armor, which

refused to be properly flexible at elbow and knee, so
that he had considerable difficulty in moving around.

Brooks Mansfield was one of Julie's favorite people, a
former diplomat and now a writer of successful and
highly esteemed books on international politics. He was a
distinguished man with a most approachable manner,
cultivated, witty, and charming. He treated Julie as
though she were his own daughter and she had frequently gone to him for advice, though he was wise
enough never to give any unasked. More than that, she
usually acted upon his suggestions as she had infinite
faith in the soundness of his judgment and the depth of
his understanding.

Dinner that evening was a gay affair. Mansfield, with
his wide range of information and social tact, always
made conversation flow easily. Bert had recovered from
whatever mood he had been in that morning, and he
had a flow of lively chatter. The Princess, as though
repentant and trying to make amends for her abruptness
in dismissing Julie so soon after her return home, was at
her radiant best.

She described the proposed transformation of May
Williams, which she was planning with the help of her
most experienced technician, breaking off to say, "By the
way, Julie, you are always begging for a job. There is
one for you. Go shopping with her, will you? She's afraid
of color and too conservative in her taste. She needs
someone to encourage her to brighten up."

"I'd love it," Julie agreed.

The Princess smiled her gratitude, and went on to
discuss a ballet she had seen recently and to exchange
banter with Mansfield about a speech he had been
snared into making. She was even more gracious than
usual to Bert Wilson. Not that she did not like him, but
she made no secret of the fact that she hoped Julie
would marry a man who had more to offer her.

There were only two subjects that weren't mentioned
at all during dinner. One was the jewel robbery; the
other, Julie's trip to Europe. Before the end of the meal
Julie had the oddest impression that she had been sent
abroad to get her out of the way, that no one seemed to

care in the least about what had happened to her during the weeks of her absence.

Actually, she thought, nothing very important had happened. She had met a man, had danced with him once, had talked with him a few times, had been warned against him. That was all. The warning had been unnecessary. No man had ever made clearer his complete indifference. She would never see him again. The very thought of it seemed to take the light out of the sky. Once she was almost unbearably tempted to tell her aunt that she had encountered Mark Sefton, whom the Princess had referred to as an insurance investigator, on shipboard, but some instinct stopped her.

As Bert was putting the black satin cape over her shoulders Julie said casually, "Oh, by the way, Aunt Georgia, I met an old friend of yours on the trip home."

"Oh? Who was that?"

"Lady Maydock."

The Princess's eyes flashed with anger. "A friend! How on earth did that woman manage to strike up an acquaintance with you?"

"We were both seated at the Captain's table. She discovered, I don't know how, that you were my aunt. She told me you were old friends."

"I barely know the woman," Aunt Georgia replied, her voice like ice.

"I should hope you don't consider her a friend!" Mansfield exclaimed. "She is an impossible creature. Married poor old Maydock, who is seventy, if he's a day, and leaves him in that moldering old country house of his in Kent for about ten months of the year. When she does pay a visit to England she spends most of her time in London. And how she managed to acquire the diamonds with which she is always plastered I can't imagine. Maydock never had two pennies to rub together. She married him for the title, I understand. So far I've been fortunate enough to remain out of her orbit. She's the kind of woman who uses people quite unscrupulously. Just as she claims your friendship, Georgia. Some people will believe that and be willing to accept her on your account."

"I trust," her aunt said to Julie, "that you didn't get

involved with the woman. In any case, you needn't see her at all in New York. She is not likely to move in the circles you know."

iii

Princess Sobelli, who was usually right about various social circles, proved, almost immediately, to be wrong about Lady Maydock.

The Princess and Julie had checked their wraps and were adjusting their masks in front of a long mirror before entering the spectacular ballroom, when a woman who had been seated on an upholstered bench before the mirror, applying lipstick lavishly, caught sight of them. She was dressed as a powder puff, with a full skirt so abbreviated it was hardly a skirt at all. She opened her evening bag, took out a gold case, and lighted a cigarette. The heavy smell of Turkish tobacco overpowered her light perfume.

"Princess Sobelli!" she exclaimed. "How delightful to see you. And your dear niece. We became acquainted on shipboard." There was a fractional pause. "I suppose she told you."

"Oh, the child is so forgetful," the Princess said. "And we've barely had time to see each other."

"I kept an eye on her for you," Lady Maydock said, and Julie had a queer feeling that the two women were saying things that had meaning for them but none for her. "You know those shipboard romances!" She saw Julie's flushed cheeks and laughed softly, crushed out her cigarette and went toward the ballroom.

The Princess stared after her. "I hope she didn't presume to introduce any of her friends to you, Julie. They aren't the kind of people you should know."

"Only one man." Julie tried to sound indifferent. "A former fiancé of hers, I think. And I barely saw him. It's unlikely I'll ever see him again."

"That's just as well. Come along, dear. Brooks and Bert will think we have forgotten them."

The huge ballroom was thronged with people in elaborate costumes. Two dance bands alternated, one for conventional dancing, one for the younger crowd. For a moment Julie watched the colorful crowd, entranced by the exotic clothes, and then Bert swept her onto the dance floor.

"One thing I never gave those old Romans credit for," he grumbled, as the music came to an end, "was managing to keep their togas on." He gave a hitch to his and Julie laughed at him.

"It's a terrific crowd," she exclaimed. "All this money goes for charity, you know. They must be really cleaning up tonight."

"The only trouble with an affair like this," Bert said, "is that the credentials of the guests aren't carefully screened, as long as they can put up fifty bucks for a ticket. No guessing who some of these people really are."

"What would you expect them to be?" she mocked him. "International spies, perhaps?"

"I was thinking of robbery," Bert answered soberly. "There's a lot of jewelry in this room tonight. And it's not so much a question of stealing it now as of tracing it to the owner's house and then choosing a safe time to move in. This ball tonight is practically an invitation to robbery."

"In that case," Julie commented, "the one to be nervous ought to be Lady Maydock."

"The one you were mentioning this evening?"

"Yes."

"Which one is she?"

"The tall fair woman dressed as a powder puff. She's simply loaded with diamonds: rings, bracelets, and a necklace."

They had arrived at the Maskers Ball at ten o'clock. After eleven, some well-known actors who had finished their evening performances began to appear. It seemed to Julie that everyone she knew, and many famous people whom she knew only because their pictures constantly appeared in the newspapers, had come to the Maskers Ball. There was a constant flash as pictures were taken of celebrities.

Bert smiled down at Julie. "Even through that mask I can see your excitement," he teased her.

"I was just thinking that it was only this morning the ship docked. Yesterday I was at sea. A week ago I was in London. And now tonight all this brilliance and excitement, all these famous people. It hardly seems real."

"It's not real," he told her. "This is a make-believe world. Behind all those masks and fancy costumes there are just ordinary people you would hardly notice. What's so exotic is only the masks they wear."

But even when, at midnight, masks were removed, the magic quality remained. Julie and Bert had been waltzing. Now a different band took over and the older group withdrew to the low balcony where spectators could watch the dancing.

Princess Sobelli, who had been dancing with Mansfield, laughed as the new rhythm started. "Not for me," she declared.

"Just a minute, Your Highness," called a photographer, and he snapped her before she and her escort started up the flight of stairs.

"Princess," cooed a woman's voice, and Lady Maydock paused beside the couple, obviously hoping that the photographer would ask for her picture too. Instead, he turned away in pursuit of a famous husband-and-wife acting team. Her lips pressed tight together and then she laughed softly. "Dear Princess, it seems so extraordinary to see you, of all people, wearing costume jewelry. They've never managed to track down your beautiful pieces, have they?"

"No, unfortunately. Perhaps they will turn up someday." The Princess, keeping a polite smile on her lips, started up the stairs without a backward look.

Lady Maydock took a step after her. "I don't believe I know your attractive escort."

"Brooks," the Princess said, "let me introduce you to Lady Maydock. Mr. Mansfield."

A hand sparkling with diamonds was extended. "Mr. Mansfield! I've heard so much about you and I've always been one of your great admirers."

"I've heard much of you too, Lady Maydock. Used to know your husband. Coming, Georgia?"

Lady Maydock stared after the retreating couple, one hand clenching in fury.

Even in that throng, Julie was recognized, hailed by her friends, though most of the group belonged to an older generation, and taken from Bert, who relinquished her, smiling. He, however, did not dance except when she was free to dance with him. There was no crowd so thick that he failed to follow with his eyes the lithe, slender figure in its scarlet and black Spanish costume, to see the high comb that held her hair.

Again the orchestras alternated, and Mansfield brought Princess Sobelli down to the dance floor. For a moment they stood near Julie and Bert. Then, as they moved forward, a man said, "Princess! How wonderful to see you again! It seems like yesterday. You haven't changed. I knew you at once."

The man was slender and he wore a dramatic black and silver harlequin costume. He had fair hair. Julie stood watching, a frown on her face, unconscious of Bert's hand on her arm.

"Don't say that you've forgotten me," the man was saying. "I'm Charles Norton, and I used to know you years ago in Florence. Your husband was a very good friend of mine."

It seemed to Julie that her aunt was curiously rigid for a moment and then she smiled. "Mr. Norton! Of course. How long ago it all seems."

"Judging by your appearance, not a day has passed," the man assured her. "And the dear old palace—with those cold marble floors. Nothing can make marble comfortable to live with, magnificent as it is." To Julie's surprise, the fair-haired man took the Princess into his arms and moved out onto the dance floor, guiding her into the colorful throng.

Mansfield turned to Julie, a scowl on his usually amiable face. "And who," he demanded, "is that man?"

"Hey, this is my dance," Bert protested, and danced away with Julie. He chuckled. "I think our Mr. Mansfield is jealous of his new competition."

"Oh, that's silly! Aunt Georgia wouldn't—that is, Mr. Mansfield is her closest friend but she isn't going to marry him. She will never marry again. Anyhow, this new man is much too young and he is—"

"He is what?" Bert demanded as Julie came to a halt.

"I don't know. There is something wrong about him."

"Step up, ladies and gentlemen," Bert chanted in mock imitation of a sideshow barker, "and have your fortunes told. The Spaniard tells all. Sees all. Knows all."

"Oh, shut up," Julie said, with the bluntness of old friendship.

"How do you know there is something wrong about the man?" Bert insisted. "If it isn't your crystal ball, is it tea leaves?"

"Go on and laugh. But didn't you notice Aunt Georgia's face? I think she is afraid of that man."

At this Bert laughed. "You crazy girl! You get some of the wildest ideas."

"Laugh if you want to, but I distrust him and I think Aunt Georgia does too."

"Well, she danced with him willingly enough."

"He just swept her onto the floor without even asking her. Maybe she had to or risk a scene, and I can't imagine Aunt Georgia doing that."

Bert laughed again. Then his expression changed. He had been looking down at Julie, and he saw her lips part in a radiant smile, saw the sudden glow in her eyes. What had brought that look into her face? What had turned a rather worried girl into this sparkling, glowing woman?

A hand tapped his shoulder and a deep voice said, "May I?"

Bert stepped back and watched Julie dance away in the arms of a tall man with black hair and broad shoulders. Instead of an elaborate costume he had simply added to his evening dress a wide red ribbon across his chest and had pinned some large tin medals on his coat.

Bert watched the couple as they danced in silence. They did not seem to speak at all. Perhaps they found words unnecessary. Julie had lifted her head and the two appeared to be studying each other gravely.

Bert felt oddly bereft. In spite of Julie's repeated refusal to marry him, he had gone on hoping. His whole life had been built around her. All his adult life. No other girl had ever attracted him. Surely that kind of faithful love would eventually bring a response. But though he was sure of her affection and her unswerving friendship, her laughing companionship and her loyalty, there had been nothing else. Never had he seen her face grow radiant at his approach, however warm her welcome might be.

The black-haired man was the one who had stood beside her at the rail of the ship. Bert remembered seeing Julie turn to speak to him but he had walked away. There had been desolation in her face and an unhappy droop to her lips. He had felt instinctively that this was a rival whom he could not defeat. And yet the man had left her. Perhaps, after all, this was only a temporary infatuation of Julie's, a shipboard romance. She would come back to him, particularly if the man was not interested in her. She had too much pride to do otherwise.

VI

The throb of the music filled the air but Julie was aware of it only through the man's sure guiding hands. They might have been alone in that great ballroom. Even when they brushed against people on the crowded floor she was not conscious of it. This moment was enough. Complete in itself.

Finally it occurred to her that he had not spoken at all beyond saying, "May I?" to Bert. She looked up at him, saw his eyes on her face, saw more clearly the curious hardness of his jaw.

"You—you left me so suddenly this morning," she said rather shyly.

"I had forgotten to prepare my list for the customs inspector," he said and she knew, without knowing how she knew, that it was not the truth. This was not a man to be careless or forgetful.

Suppose, she thought in a panic, he does not ask whether he can see me again. Suppose after this dance he—just goes away as he did when we danced on the ship and again this morning. Goes without a word. Sometimes it was hard to be a woman. A woman had to wait to be asked. A man could ask—or not. The choice was his.

The choice was his. Only that morning she had assured May Williams blithely that a woman could win any man she wanted, if she used her head. She knew now that it was not true. There was something electric and wonderful that bound her to this man and then, unexpectedly, there was a barrier, like a curtain of steel that came down between them, that could not be crossed.

The music stopped. Mark dropped her hand and

53

stepped back. He was going to take her to Bert. And then she heard her aunt's voice beside her saying, "Of course I remember very well now how you and Dino used to play with that tremendous chess set of his."

Julie turned eagerly. "Aunt Georgia, do let me present a shipboard acquaintance. Mr. Sefton. My aunt, Princess Sobelli." She looked quickly from one unrevealing face to the other.

"How do you do, Mr. Sefton."

"This is a pleasure, Princess."

There was no indication that they had ever met before. Then her aunt said, rather reluctantly, Julie thought, "Julie, I don't believe you know Mr. Norton. My niece, Miss Bryce. And Mr. Sefton."

The two men bowed. Neither of them extended his hand. Then Mark looked gravely at Julie. "Thank you for the dance." He melted into the crowd.

"Haven't I seen you before?" Julie asked the fair-haired man.

He shook his head. "It can't be. I wouldn't have forgotten you." There was a practiced flattery in his voice that she disliked. He appeared to have a low opinion of women, to assume they all succumbed to compliments which they must know to be artificial.

"That's odd. I would have sworn that, just a few weeks ago, I saw you near my aunt's palace in Florence, and that you directed me back to my hotel."

Julie saw her aunt's hand tighten on the carved ivory fan she was carrying. The smile seemed to have frozen on her lips.

Then Mansfield was claiming the Princess for a dance and Norton smiled at Julie. "Will you?"

He danced well, better than anyone she had ever danced with before, almost like a professional. He had the kind of assurance that made his partner feel that she too was a superb dancer. Unlike Mark, he talked lightly and gaily. "So you've just come from Florence. Lucky girl! I haven't been there in many years. As I was just reminding your aunt, her husband was a friend and mentor long ago. It was wonderful to see her again. She never changes, does she?"

"Not very much."

"How long were you in Italy?"

It seemed strange to Julie that her aunt was without any interest in her trip and yet people like Mark Sefton and Lady Maydock and now this man Charles Norton wanted to know about it to the last detail. Exhausted by his probing questions, she was relieved when Bert came to claim her.

Norton relinquished her with a smile. "I'll be seeing you again, Miss Bryce. Seeing you often, I hope."

She smiled vaguely and turned with relief to Bert.

"I had a kind of idea," he said casually, "that you wanted to get away from that guy."

"I did," she agreed, "but how did you guess?"

"I know you so well." There was something wistful in the smile he gave her. "Come along and take a look at this." He led her out of the ballroom and down a narrow corridor, flung open the door of a room which was apparently used as a small cocktail lounge but was now deserted. The lights were dim. On three sides there were walls of glass looking out and down on one of the most terrific sights in the world, the panorama of Manhattan at night, a brilliant spectacle that lights up the sky.

"Oh," she cried out in delight. "Oh!"

"Julie," Bert said, and there was no trace of his usual gaiety, "I love you very much. I've asked you this many times before. Will you marry me?"

"Oh, Bert! Please, Bert!" Something in his voice made her grieve, as she never had before, at the pain she was inflicting.

He smiled at her. "All right, honey. It's all right. I've been making a nuisance of myself for a long time. Much too long a time. I should have known that you would never have me. No reason on earth why you would give me a thought. But tonight I know at least why you won't. I think I knew this morning."

Her big eyes opened wider than ever while she looked at him in surprise.

"I saw your face when you were at the rail of the ship, looking after that black-haired guy. I saw it again when he asked you to dance tonight."

Color rose in a flood into Julie's cheeks but she met his

eyes without wavering. "I'm sorry, Bert. There's just
nothing I can do about it."

"And you're too honest to lie." He smiled again. "That's
one of the things I love you for. I'm proud of you,
honey. I just have two more things to say. One, I won't
propose again. Two, I'll always be around if you need
me or want me—if there's any chance of that. You've
become kind of a habit with me. But I won't call you. It
will be easier if I don't see you too often."

"Oh, Bert!" Her eyes glistened with tears and there
was a lump in her throat when she tried to swallow.

"It's all right, honey. Everything is all right as long as
you're happy."

She slipped her hand in his and they stood, hand in
hand, staring out at the dazzling panorama, neither of
them even aware of it. From where they stood, in deep
shadow, they could barely be seen. The eye instinctively
went to that incredible display of lights beyond the
windows, not to the shadows within.

Julie did not realize that they were not alone until she
smelled Turkish tobacco. She turned her head sharply. A
man and a woman had just entered the room. The
woman's powder-puff costume was unmistakable. She
reached for an ashtray to crush out her cigarette, her
hand gleaming with diamonds. Then she was in the
arms of her escort.

"Mark!" she said. "What a fool I was! We belong
together. Oh, Mark!"

Julie's hand tightened convulsively on Bert's. Moving
as noiselessly as the shadows they seemed to be, they
went out of the cocktail lounge and back to the music
and the laughter and the excitement of the ballroom.
Julie's face was white but her head was high. Bert was
careful not to look at her, though her face revealed
nothing of her bewilderment and her pain.

The crowd was beginning to thin out. Now it was
possible to recognize more people: movie stars, flamboy-
ant in exotic costumes; musical comedy actresses with
their current escorts; diplomats and their wives; a much-
photographed model escorted by a much-married bank-
er; social friends of Princess Sobelli's and the younger
generation known chiefly to Julie.

Princess Sobelli was dancing with a French diplomat, a man known for the gravity of his manner, contrasted by his clown's costume and a chalk-white face with a wide smile painted on it.

"Julie, save an old man's pride," Mansfield grunted from beside her.

She managed a laugh. "You! An old man?"

"It's not age, it's this confounded armor. Every time I dance I manage to get tangled up and hit someone. I've never appreciated those knights of old. Imagine fighting in this stuff! Or riding a horse. Anyhow, I've had enough dancing for one night. Your aunt seems just to be getting started."

"Let's sit this one out," Julie suggested soothingly, and they went up to the balcony. She turned back to wave at Bert but he was not, for once, looking after her. He was leaning against the wall, looking down at his feet. His very shoulders sagged with discouragement and she longed to comfort him, but the only comfort he needed she could not provide. Not even with the searing memory of the tall slim woman in the abbreviated powder-puff costume in Mark's arms.

When they were seated, Mansfield said, with a scowl which was unlike him, "Who is that fellow who's been hanging around Georgia tonight?"

"His name is Norton. Charles Norton. He says he is an old friend of Dino Sobelli's and he says that he knew Aunt Georgia years ago."

Something in her tone alerted Mansfield. "Says?" he repeated sharply.

"I don't believe him," Julie said. "Bert laughed at me for playing a hunch or something, but I don't like the man and I don't trust him."

"Surely Georgia would know whether or not the man had been a friend of Dino's and of hers."

"Well, she said she did. But I heard her make some comment about how he and Dino used to play chess and I remember how she told me once, laughing, that Dino had never been able even to remember the chess moves. So that much, at least, was not true."

Again there was that undercurrent in Julie's voice. Mansfield reached out, took her chin in his hand, turned

her to face him. "Look here, my dear, you know how I
feel about your aunt. If something is wrong, you can tell
me."

"But I don't know that anything is wrong. I just—feel
it. Bert says it's crystal gazing or tea leaves or something. I call it instinct."

"Instinct is not a bad thing to follow. Can you tell me
exactly what worries you?" As she hesitated, he added
quietly, "I do not need to explain that all I want is to
serve your aunt. I won't abuse your confidence."

Julie nodded. "The trouble is that I don't really know
anything but—well, here it is." She started with Bert's
suspicions about the jewel robbery. In his newspaper
circles he had heard persistent rumors that the Sobelli
business was on the rocks and that her aunt had to raise
money and was having difficulty in doing so. Bert believed that the jewel robbery had been faked to defraud
the insurance company.

When Mansfield started to protest, Julie rushed on to
tell him what she had overheard of her aunt's conversation with Mark Sefton, whom she had explained as
being an insurance investigator, though the ship's
officer, who knew him, was sure that was not the case.
Tonight, her aunt and Mark Sefton had met as total
strangers.

"I met him myself," Mansfield commented. "He was
dancing with the wife of one of the Cabinet members.
Impressive-looking chap. Well, it's an odd story, though
there is probably a simple explanation."

"I know, but that isn't all," Julie told him and she
went on to describe her encounter outside the Sobelli
palace in Florence with Charles Norton, who now declared that he had not been in Italy for years.

"I suppose you are quite sure about meeting him,"
Mansfield said. "There are cases of strong resemblances,
you know, and he isn't an unusual type."

"I am positive. Not just his looks and the way he
moves but particularly his voice. And he recognized me.
I could tell by a kind of flicker in his eyes when he saw
me tonight. He wasn't pleased about it. And there is
more than that. While the caretaker was guiding me
through the palace I kept smelling Turkish tobacco. As

you know, I have never smoked so I have a keen sense of smell. Once we had a game of guessing kinds of tobacco by the smell and I always won. So I'm sure about this. And it sounded—I thought I heard someone in the palace at the time. And the caretaker is afraid of the place; he thinks it's haunted. And he hears things too."

Mansfield smiled at that and Julie clutched at his arm, her fingers slipping on the metallic armor.

"It's not funny and it's not just my imagination." She told him about her cabin on shipboard having been searched, and that there had again been a scent of Turkish tobacco.

Mansfield adjusted one of the tin pieces that covered a knee and crossed his legs with some difficulty and a great deal of clanking. "Was this fellow Norton on shipboard?"

"I didn't see him. I'm pretty sure he couldn't have been or we would have been bound to encounter each other at some time."

"And you are positive that you did not imagine the Turkish tobacco. Well, let's look at the other possibilities. Have you any ideas?"

Seeing that he was taking her alarm seriously, Julie felt her heart lift in relief. "Lady Maydock smokes Turkish cigarettes and she was very much in evidence on shipboard. She practically hounded me after she learned from someone that I was related to Aunt Georgia. And tonight—were you there when she was making those snide remarks about Aunt Georgia's jewelry being fake?"

There was a long silence. Then Mansfield said thoughtfully, "I'll look into this thing, Julie. We won't discuss it with anyone. But if Georgia should be in trouble—and yet," he broke off, "in that case, why wouldn't she have come to me? She must know that I would help."

"What do you think you can do?"

He smiled down at the earnest, trusting face. "It's— good heavens, it's half-past three and you've had a long day and probably didn't sleep much last night in your excitement about getting home. I had better collect your aunt and you can collect your young man."

"Not her young man, alas," Bert said from behind them. He grinned reassuringly at Julie. "The Princess asked me to find you. It's getting late." His grin broadened, was almost the gay one to which Julie was accustomed. "You lucky ones can sleep in the morning but I am a poor galley slave and my alarm goes off at six o'clock."

As Mansfield followed Julie down the stairs, he said, "You asked me what I can do. I don't know, but I'll think of something. Trust me, Julie."

ii

At half-past four that morning Julie got out of bed. It was hopeless to try to sleep. Whenever she closed her eyes a whole series of unanswered, unanswerable questions stormed her defenseless mind. Why had her aunt pretended not to know Mark Sefton? Why had she pretended to know Charles Norton? Why had Lady Maydock seemed to be talking on two levels to her aunt? What did she know about the missing jewelry? And why had Mark Sefton taken Lady Maydock into his arms? Did he love her? What had the woman said about him to Julie? Something about the fact that they had nearly married but that she had been afraid. Now, apparently, she had changed her mind.

Julie slipped her feet into pale green satin slippers, drew on a matching robe of soft velvet, went to open her door. Down below there was the unmistakable tap of a high heel on a bare floor. Her aunt always wore high heels, even on bedroom slippers, and she had scatter rugs on the floor of her private sitting room, which was directly under Julie's own bedroom.

Julie hesitated at the head of the stairs, heard the restless heel tap again. Her aunt must be awake and pacing the floor. She ran softly down the stairs and knocked at the door.

"Who is it?" her aunt asked, startled.

"Julie."

"Oh." There was a moment's hesitation. Then her aunt said, rather reluctantly, "Well, come in, child."

The second-floor suite, Princess Sobelli's private living quarters, was as luxurious as the rest of the town house. At the back of the house, above the dining room, was the bedroom with its canopied bed, its silver gray carpet, and soft green velvet chairs and draperies. The dressing table had come from a Parisian antique shop; the chairs were Florentine, probably from the palace. The crystal bottles on the dressing table were museum pieces and contained a whole array of cosmetics.

The bathroom had a sunken tub and a pink marble floor. The sitting room, on the front of the house, was done in colors ranging from the golden brown of the scatter rugs to gold upholstery and hangings, and to a pale yellow ceiling. There was an Empire sofa which might well have been in an old French château, deep soft chairs were drawn up before the fireplace with its Adam mantelpiece, an inlaid desk was lighted by a priceless lamp. On the walls were Impressionist paintings.

Princess Sobelli was wrapped in a gold velvet robe to match her surroundings. Otherwise she was at odds with them. There was little trace of the glamorous woman of a few hours earlier. Her hair was pinned in place to control its wave and covered by a thick net. Her face had a heavy mask of cold cream. There were wrinkle-eradicators on her forehead and a chin strap was tied under her jaw and over her head.

In spite of herself Julie giggled and her aunt smiled reluctantly.

"Ridiculous, isn't it?" she admitted. "But it gets results." She caught sight of herself in a long mirror and joined spontaneously in Julie's laughter. "If only Brooks could see me now, that would cure him of his romantic illusions."

"I doubt it. His devotion isn't skin deep, Aunt Georgia. He really adores you."

"I know. I've tried to make him see that it is useless. Honestly I have, Julie. I hate the idea of keeping him dangling but somehow he just hangs on. He won't give up. He thinks eventually I'll turn to him, even though I told him tonight—"

"You refused that poor man again tonight?" Julie asked.

Her aunt nodded.

"And yet," Julie began. Hesitated.

"And yet?" her aunt prompted.

"I wonder what you would do without him. He is always there, always to be depended on. Not simply as an escort but as a friend. Loyal and reliable and wonderful company. It's a lonely thing to be a solitary woman."

"I know that. Better than you, perhaps. But I don't like to cling."

"Of course you don't."

"And while you are speaking for my poor Brooks, what about Bert?"

There was a reluctant half smile on Julie's lips. "I know. I told him tonight it was no use, and he said he would never ask me again but that he would always be there if I wanted him."

The Princess, who was usually so disciplined and controlled that she appeared to be in complete repose, got up restlessly to pace the floor.

Julie watched her for some time in silence. This was the first time the two women had ever talked so frankly of their personal affairs, but neither of them seemed to find it strange. Their thoughts followed different tracks and neither of them was pleasant.

At last Julie said, "Mr. Mansfield didn't like that man Norton, Aunt Georgia."

Her aunt paused, the tips of one hand resting on a table. Her shoulders were rigid. She did not move, did not even seem to breathe. At length she said casually, "Really? I thought he seemed rather amusing."

"Just the same, he lied when he said he had not been in Italy for a long time. I did see him outside your palace in Florence. I know I did. I couldn't be mistaken. And, what's more, he had been in the palace ahead of me. At least I am pretty sure he had. He was smoking Turkish tobacco and I could smell it in the palace."

"What on earth," the Princess demanded, "were you doing in the palace?"

"I'd never even seen it," Julie reminded her. "The few times I've gone to Italy I've spent my time in Rome or Venice. And I was curious because I have always heard so much about it."

Her aunt swallowed, spoke with difficulty. "How did you get in?"

"Oh, your caretaker, Giuseppe, showed me around when I told him who I was."

Her aunt seemed to relax a little, though her fingers still pressed hard on the table as though helping to support her weight. "Perhaps Giuseppe smokes Turkish tobacco."

"Giuseppe wasn't smoking and he doesn't go through the rooms of the palace at all if he can avoid it. He thinks the palace is haunted."

"As I remember, he was always rather a fool. I suppose the place is simply disintegrating."

"It's pretty bad," Julie agreed.

"Restoration isn't practicable. I've been thinking of giving it to the Italian government, in case they care to have it as an historical landmark." A jeweled clock chimed softly. "Five o'clock!" the Princess said. "You must get to bed and sleep, Julie." She rubbed her fingers over her forehead and then reached for tissues to wipe away the grease. "And so must I. It seems weeks and weeks since I have been able to sleep properly."

Julie pulled herself wearily out of the deep comfortable chair in which she had been sunk. "Aunt Georgia," she asked quickly, before her courage could fail her, "why did you act tonight as though you had never met Mr. Sefton before?"

It was a stranger with a cold, almost a hard, face who looked back at her. "You are being rude, Julie."

Julie's driving need to learn the truth was stronger than her fear of annoying her aunt. Too much was happening that she did not understand. She had the curious and unpleasant impression that she was being manipulated like a puppet. She felt sure now that the whole elaborate business of the European trip had been an attempt to get her out of the way, that she had upset someone's calculations by her visit to the palace, and that in some queer way her aunt and Lady Maydock and Charles Norton and Mark Sefton were linked together. Some very queer way, because none of them seemed even to like each other. Except Mark and Lady Maydock, locked in each other's arms. She must drive that memory out of her mind. Or perhaps she would be wise to remember it.

"I have to know, Aunt Georgia. I am positive that Mark Sefton is the one who came to see you the day after the robbery, the man you told me was an insurance investigator."

Princess Sobelli's voice was almost harsh and there was a hint of panic in it. "Never say that again to anyone. Anyone, Julie. Do you understand me?"

Julie's knees were shaking and she sank down on the broad arm of the chair for support. "Aunt Georgia," she asked, her voice steady, though her heart was thumping like an African drum, "are you doing something dangerous?"

And then the Princess turned to face her. "Yes, I am."

Julie's hands clutched each other. "Is it for money?"

"I would do anything—I have a reason for what I am doing. That is all I can tell you."

"Aren't you afraid?"

"Horribly," the Princess said. "But that won't stop me."

VII

While Julie and her aunt were talking in the Sobelli town house on Park Avenue, Bert was talking to Brooks Mansfield in the latter's terrace apartment on Central Park South.

All four had appeared to be exhausted when they left the Maskers Ball and they had done little talking in the taxi that took the two women home. Naturally, the fact that both men had been rejected by the women they loved had left them in a state of emotional depression.

When the Princess and Julie had gone into the house Mansfield raised his brows. "May I give you a lift?"

"Would I be imposing if I asked you to let me talk to you for a while, sir?" Bert asked. "I know it is terribly late but—"

The older man studied the younger one, the flaming red hair, the engaging face with its direct eyes and humorous mouth. At the moment, however, there was no trace of the usual smile.

"Of course. Will you come along to my place?"

"I'd appreciate it."

The apartment had a huge living room. There was a cream rug and cream walls on which hung modern paintings, abstractions that provided great splashes of violent color, reds and greens and golds and blues. Near the fireplace there was a love seat in crimson leather. There were crimson draperies framing the great window that filled nearly the entire north wall and looked out on a garden and down upon the darkness of Central Park below, framed on either side by the lights of Fifth Avenue and Central Park West.

For a moment Bert stood at the window, entranced, and then he took the chair the older man offered him.

"Well?" Mansfield asked. Then he saw the sudden

quirk of amusement on Bert's lips and realized how absurd he must appear in his tin suit of armor. "Here, I'll get rid of this thing. Be back in a few minutes."

When he returned, wearing a smoking jacket, he stretched out in a big chair and filled his pipe slowly.

"All right. Let's have it."

"It's that man Norton," Bert told him. "None of my business, of course, but there's something wrong about him. Julie thinks so too."

"What do you imagine is wrong?"

"I'm afraid that he has some hold on the Princess."

"I didn't care much for the man either," Mansfield said. "It probably doesn't concern either of us," and he smiled at the anxious young newspaperman who was watching him, "but I have ways of getting information. I'll see what I can find out about the fellow."

"Thank you, sir."

"What," Mansfield asked unexpectedly, "is really worrying you, young man? Oh, I share your opinion that something is definitely wrong as far as Norton is concerned, but I can't see you getting all hot and bothered about Princess Sobelli and her problems."

Bert flushed, hitched up the absurd toga, too absorbed in his worries to be conscious of the ridiculous appearance he made.

"If it is any help," Mansfield said quietly, "Julie trusts me and confides in me. As a matter of fact, she spoke to me about Norton tonight."

"If she confided in you," Bert said, "you know that I haven't a chance with her. I'm not kicking about that. In a way, I never really believed she could love me. I suppose no guy could help hoping when he meets a girl like that, but—well, that part is over."

Mansfield raised an eyebrow. He waited patiently.

"Julie is in love, sir. Really in love. Gone right off the deep end. And I'm worried."

"Why?"

"Because he—to begin with, the man is playing around with another woman."

"The hell he is!" Mansfield was angry. Then he looked at Bert. "Sure you aren't being misled by jealousy?" He held up a hand. "Oh, that would be natural enough. I wouldn't blame you for that, but jealousy does distort reason."

"Reason, perhaps, but not evidence. I wasn't misled when both Julie and I saw a woman in his arms tonight. And the woman was Lady Maydock, who should be called the Queen of Diamonds, judging by the number she wears."

"That woman!" Mansfield snorted in disgust. He puffed silently at his pipe for a thoughtful minute. "There is something about Julie; I thought she had more—well, a sounder instinct about people. But the kind of man who would fall for the obvious wiles of a woman like Lady Maydock isn't worthy of Julie. Who is this fellow, Bert?"

"I don't know."

"But I thought you knew him. You say you saw him."

"Oh, I've seen him but I don't know anything about him. His name is Mark Sefton. I think you met him tonight. And he was on the ship when Julie came home. I don't," Bert swallowed, "want Julie hurt, sir."

"Neither do I. Though I must say if she stays in love with the man after seeing him with the Maydock woman, I'll be greatly disappointed in her."

The great clock at Columbus Circle showed five o'clock. Bert got up. "I didn't mean to keep you so long."

"Any time, my boy. Julie is like my own daughter, and Georgia—well, she is now, as she has been for many years, the one woman."

Bert grinned shyly. "I know, sir, we're two guys in the same boat." Then he flushed at his temerity.

For a moment Mansfield was startled and then he smiled and laid a friendly hand on Bert's shoulder as they walked to the door.

"So we are. You aren't going to get much sleep, are you?"

"Oh, I won't even try to go to bed now. I'll go home and change out of these fool clothes and walk to work. That may wake me up. Good night, sir, and thank you."

ii

Five o'clock. The city that never slept was at least dozing. There were few sounds except for the swish of

tires of an occasional taxi, the rumble of all-night trucking, the blood-chilling sound of a distant siren. The
cocktail lounge in her hotel had long since closed and
Lady Maydock and Charles Norton had moved out into
the lobby. Except for a weary porter emptying ashtrays,
a sleepy night clerk at the desk, and a uniformed bell-
hop dozing behind the counter, the place was deserted.

Earlier there had been a few hotel guests, returning
from late parties or nightclubs, who had looked with
interest at the two exotic figures: the harlequin in black
and silver and the slim woman with the abbreviated
fluffy skirt, her neck and arms and fingers glittering with
diamonds.

"You are a fool to wear all that stuff," Norton commented bluntly. "Aside from the fact that it makes you
look like a jeweler's display counter, it's just asking for
trouble. Some dark night you're going to be held up."

Lady Maydock laughed. "In that case, I can always
collect on my insurance." Norton joined in her laughter.
"Anyhow, there is no satisfaction in having diamonds if
you can't wear them."

"The trouble with you," he said insolently, "is that you
want to be accepted socially and yet you do the things
that aren't acceptable. That's why I say you're a fool."

"Speaking of fools—and don't overestimate my pa-
tience when you do that, my dear Charles—you were a
fool, a prize fool, when you were careless enough to let
that girl see you in Florence."

He shrugged. "If you can figure out how I could have
avoided it, I wish you would tell me. I'd just unloaded
the stuff and locked the closet, and then that idiotic
Giuseppe started going through the palace, room by
room, with Julie Bryce. It took me a good fifteen minutes to figure out who she was and why she was there
and meanwhile I was darting around corners to keep out
of her sight. Because if some stranger was being allowed
the run of the palace, I had to know it."

"And just why was Miss Bryce there?" Lady Maydock
asked, her voice like a cat's purr.

"Well, of course, she's the Princess's niece and she was
just looking the place over out of curiosity."

"Sometimes I think you are rather naïve, Charles. You're taking for granted that the Princess hasn't told her the truth. This is the first time the girl has ever shown an interest in the Sobelli palace. Are you ready to swear that it was just coincidence that she was sent abroad at this time? Could you swear it was just idle curiosity that took her to the palace? Has it occurred to you that the Princess is a businesswoman and she may have sent little Bryce as her emissary to check on you?"

Norton was tired and irritable. The woman's air of mocking assurance annoyed him. Nonetheless, he made no immediate retort; he tried to curb his temper. Only trouble could come of quarreling with her at this point. When the job was done he would get out and stay out. He hoped devoutly he would never see her again. But he could not afford to cause a break now. He had invested too much time and effort; he had taken too many chances. At this hour of the morning, when vitality was at its lowest ebb, it did not pay to think about the chances he had taken. This was no time to lose his nerve.

He spoke with more confidence than he felt. "If there was any other reason, I'll eat my hat."

"It might give you indigestion. I can tell you one thing, my self-confident friend. Julie Bryce met Mark Sefton on the ship and fell head over heels in love with him."

"Just who is Mark Sefton?"

"I've never been quite sure," Lady Maydock said slowly. "He keeps cropping up in the most unexpected way and in the most unexpected places. He's the most attractive man I've ever met and the most elusive. Once I nearly married him but—I changed my mind."

Norton's eyes narrowed as he looked at her. "I always know when you're lying, Lisa, and that's lucky for me, isn't it? I'd be willing to bet a thousand to one that he turned you down."

She glared at him, the hand with its glittering jewels turned into claws, curling as though to scratch. Then, aware of his thinly veiled mockery, she relaxed and smiled at him lazily. "All right, my friend. Have it your own way. But I spiked Julie Bryce's guns tonight. I let her get a good look at me in Mark's arms. That ought to change any ideas she has been building. I have a strong suspicion that it would be dangerous to let those two get together and—shall we say, exchange confidences."

"Judging by what I saw of him tonight, it's just possible you are fighting outside your own weight class, Lisa," he drawled. "It might not be healthy to interfere with him or to make trouble for the girl, just in case he is interested in her. And it could be easy to be interested in her. Very easy. She's lovely, Lisa. That's a warning."

"Then let me warn you that the chief danger you are facing at this moment is not that Giuseppe might let someone examine that locked closet in the Sobelli palace in Florence. After all, big as the loss would be, it couldn't involve us directly. We would be safe enough. No, the chief danger is a girl named Julie Bryce, right here in Manhattan. If her aunt has confided in her, she's a real danger, Charles. You can't afford to make any mistakes. *Any* mistakes. Is that clear?"

"That's clear enough," he said sullenly. "But if she gets unmanageable I should think your best course would be to tell the Princess. She will keep the girl in line. She'll have to. Otherwise, I'll handle her myself."

"What does that mean?"

His rather shallow eyes met hers without expression. "Just what you think it does, my dear Lisa. This deal runs into millions. No girl is going to get in my way. If she tries, it will be the last thing she does."

For the first time he had the deep satisfaction of feeling stronger than Lisa Maydock. He had frightened her. Good!

"By the way," he asked, "what percentage does the Princess expect?"

Lady Maydock got to her feet. She had shaken off that moment of fear. It was absurd to be afraid of Charles, who was actually a coward. For some reason, it did not occur to her that nothing is more dangerous than a cornered rat. She yawned. "She expects more than she has any chance of collecting. It's nearly six o'clock. Better get out of here."

VIII

In the cloakroom, Mark pulled off the broad red ribbon and the tin medals and tossed them into a wastebasket. He carefully buttoned a lightweight raincoat over his evening clothes, turned up the collar to conceal his white tie, waited for a moment while a noisy group was leaving, and drifted along in their wake.

Some of them were waiting for their own cars, others were trying to hail taxis, still others were walking away, hoping to have less competition for transportation a few blocks farther on.

After some three blocks Mark dropped a handkerchief, bent down to retrieve it, and looked behind him and across the street. No one seemed to be paying any attention to him.

He dived into the nearest subway entrance, clattered down the stairs and out onto the platform. Aside from a drunk asleep on a bench there was no one in sight. Nonetheless he instinctively stayed away from the edge of the platform. Even drunks had been known to sober up with amazing speed when there was an opportunity to attack Mark Sefton.

When a train finally rumbled into the station, the drunk did not stir. Looking quickly up and down the platform, Mark noticed that no one else boarded the train and, for the first time since he had left the ball, he relaxed.

There were only half a dozen passengers in the car with him, most of them half asleep, a few reading newspapers or working crossword puzzles.

Mark left the train at Times Square, waiting until the other passengers had preceded him, and then hastened

71

upstairs, followed the green line to the shuttle for Grand Central Station.

He made his way along corridors and went toward the big circular information booth in the upper level of the station. A man in overalls was looking at a timetable. Mark stopped beside him and reached for a timetable from the rack.

"Hotel Commodore, room 909," the workman said without raising his eyes from the timetable.

"Thanks," Mark said, looking at the counter. He paused to fill the pipe he carried in his pocket, taking his time, looking around him casually. He noticed everything and everyone in that apparently idle gaze: a tired cleaner pushing a broom ahead of him; a tired mother with two small sleeping children on a bench; a thin trickle of passengers coming from an early train. No one seemed to be interested in Mark Sefton.

He was tempted to stop for coffee but he was late enough as it was and the meeting must have been going on for hours, discussing ways and means, thrashing out various problems, looking at new evidence. Not that Mark minded missing that. He liked action but he became restless in long meetings. There was, he contended, too much talk, too much going over possibilities, too much weighing alternatives, too much repetition of the same ideas.

The elevator door slid open on the ninth floor of the Commodore, and Mark walked down the hall looking for room 909. He tapped on it lightly. No one in that room would be likely to want any attention drawn to the meeting.

The door was opened almost at once by a quiet, nondescript-looking young man. "Come in, Sefton, we've been waiting half the night for you."

"Hello, Chambers. Hi there, Fosdick. Sorry to keep you so long, Mr. Harris. I got held up." While he was speaking he tossed his raincoat onto a chair.

"So I see," the man named Harris remarked smoothly. He leaned forward and removed a long blond hair from Mark's shoulder. "Held up," he remarked to the grinning men.

Mark grinned back without embarrassment. "Just part of the hazards of the job."

"And what hazard was this, if I may ask?"

"That's Lady Maydock's hair, and Lady Maydock is in this."

"How far?"

"My guess," Mark said slowly, "is all the way. But I don't know. Wherever I go I keep finding traces of her but I can't lay my hands on any proof. It's maddening."

"You really think she is one of them?"

"I'd be inclined to guess that she's head of the whole organization."

"You have a talent for putting a finger on the important feature of every case, Mark. So I take it that this little interlude," and Harris, who sat at the head of the table, touched the blond hair which he had laid on the polished mahogany, "was what held you up."

"It was one of the things, sir," Mark said evenly. "Don't make any mistake about it. Lady Maydock is no more interested in me as a man than I am in her as a woman. She is extremely interested in my job. She has never stopped trying to find out what I really do. Sometimes I think she suspects, that she is on the right track."

"How did you come across her in the first place?"

"Pure accident, so far as I know. A few years ago, I met her casually at some big affair like the one tonight, where credentials aren't too carefully scrutinized; some charity deal, I think. She hadn't married Maydock then, poor old devil. At her pressing invitation I called on her a few times and took her out to dinner. Then I shied off."

"Why?"

"She never stopped digging for information."

"But tonight you thought she was important enough to keep us waiting for hours."

"Let's say that she thought I was worth it. And again it was no tribute to my charms. And there were things, intangibles." He beat his clenched fist lightly on the table. "I can't get anything tangible. But the woman is loaded with diamonds and Maydock certainly didn't provide them. Nor do I believe she got them because of her—persuasive charms."

"Well, what do you think?"

"She'd be afraid of having too much cash around. Have to declare it for income tax, for one thing. For another, money arouses curiosity and awkward questions when it comes too suddenly and from no visible source. No, I think those diamonds represent her share of whatever she is mixed up in. Though she is shrewd enough in other ways, she is just sufficiently foolish to flaunt them. She simply can't resist wearing them. She carries a fortune in diamonds around on her, at least in the evenings. I don't suppose even Lady Maydock decks out in jewelry of that kind in the daytime."

"Have you anything against her except the diamonds and her interest in you?" asked the quiet young man named Chambers.

"Intangibles, again. She is practically stalking Princess Sobelli." The three men stiffened as he spoke of her. "She was on the ship on which I came back—good Lord, was that only yesterday morning?—and Julie Bryce, the Princess's niece, was on the same ship. After she found out who the girl was, the Maydock woman followed her as closely as the tail on a cat. She also searched the girl's cabin, but if she found anything I can't imagine where she hid it, recalling how she was dressed at the time."

"I take it you were watching her."

"I was watching her," Mark said grimly.

"Do you think the Bryce girl is involved in this?" Fosdick, a large, good-humored-looking man with hard eyes, demanded.

"No, I'm sure she doesn't have the faintest idea what it is all about. She is completely in the clear and she has got to be kept that way."

Something in Sefton's voice drew the three pairs of eyes to his face in intense scrutiny.

"What makes you so sure she is in the clear?" Harris asked.

"I talked to her about her European trip. She told me about her aunt's business and the new designs for packaging of cosmetics and how she had visited the old Sobelli palace and what a pity it was that the place should be so run down. She wasn't holding out any information. She is as clear as crystal. Transparently honest."

There was silence in the room for some time. Then Harris telephoned room service and ordered coffee for four. It was Fosdick who broke the silence.

"What about the Princess's jewelry?"

"It's in my safety-deposit box," Mark told him.

"No trouble with the police or the insurance people?"

"Well, there was some, of course. They didn't like it. I've never talked harder in trying to sell an unpopular idea."

"You can hardly expect they would like playing our game for us," Harris commented.

"I finally persuaded them that winning the game was important to all of us."

"We haven't won it yet. How long is this thing going on?" Chambers asked.

"I think it is about ready to break," Mark told him. "The longer they wait now, the greater the risk of discovery. Someone may get curious and break open a locked closet in the Sobelli palace ahead of time. Even that fool Giuseppe might want to know what is going on. Anyhow, the new Sobelli lipsticks and perfume and compacts are due to be shipped very shortly. We'll know, of course, the moment they are moved, and we'll be ready to go into action."

"And what are the chances that they'll get here safely?"

"Excellent, I think." Mark emptied his pipe into an ash tray. "Excellent. We'll never have our eyes off them. The idea of smuggling dope in cosmetics is clever. When rumors got abroad that Princess Sobelli's business was on the rocks, someone was bound to think she would be the right person to approach. Then, of course, that jewel robbery in which no one believed—and I will say that her response to our suggestion was incredible. She was not only willing, she was eager to play along with us."

"Does she realize that she could be in danger?" Fosdick asked. "There is more than five million dollars' worth of the stuff coming in, as we figure it. People don't pull their punches for that kind of money. They kill for it."

"She knows."

"And you think she will go through with it, that she won't break? At this point that could mean disaster. The stuff would never get here. It would be moved in such a way that we would never get track of it again, never pin these people down. And you know as well as I do what that would mean."

Mark's face was grim. "She'll go through with it. As I said, she is willing to accept any danger involved. It is quite possible that this may be one of the biggest dope-smuggling operations ever. For the Princess the personal danger is, apparently, worthwhile. But her niece Julie may also be in danger and she is not aware of it, and she has not been asked to say whether or not she is willing to accept the risks involved. I suggest that something adequate be done at once for her protection."

"That's up to the Princess, isn't it? She can send the girl away someplace."

"She did send her to Europe," Mark pointed out, "but she couldn't keep her there without some sort of explanation. And the girl just chanced to go to the palace at the very time when Norton was there. God knows what he made of it! I saw him tonight, by the way, establishing contact with the Princess. He acted as though he had never seen Miss Bryce before. I only hope she didn't see him at the palace; that would really put her in danger."

"The Princess will simply have to arrange to look after the girl."

"And where," Mark demanded, "do you think Miss Bryce would be safe if Norton believed she had any knowledge of the racket and how it is being handled?" The strain in his voice was clear to all the men; so were the lines of anxiety in his face.

"Look here," Harris said, "you've been working without a break since this thing came up. As soon as it's over you had better take a leave of absence."

"And meantime," Mark said insistently, "what happens to Julie Bryce?"

"I'm sorry, Sefton," Harris said quietly. "I didn't realize that you were personally involved with the girl."

"I'm not," Mark said. "I'm not personally involved with any woman. In my job I don't dare to be. No woman wants to marry a man who may be shot or stabbed or poisoned or dumped into the East River with his feet encased in cement. When I took on this job I knew what I was doing. I'm not complaining about that. I have no time for love in my life. But this girl—nothing must happen to her."

"I sometimes wonder," Harris said, responding to the torture in Mark's voice rather than to his actual words, "if anyone knows how much is expected of the men in our department. Everyone is aware of what a soldier or sailor or marine or pilot is up against, what chances he takes, what danger he runs, but we are the invisible men in the background, the men without identity and without faces, who try to keep things safe and decent and law-abiding at home. And some of us run greater risks than a man does under fire. In fact, we are under fire all the time. I'm sorry, Sefton."

"I'm not complaining."

"It's another day," Harris said, looking at his watch. "Nothing can happen for a few days at least. We can all afford to relax. Get out in the country, Sefton. What's your favorite sport?"

"Riding; I have a ranch in Montana with a fine man to run it for me. Of course, I don't manage to get out there very often."

Harris grinned. "Swallow your pride and rent a hack and ride in Central Park," he advised. "It might help you to blow away the cobwebs."

"That's an idea," Mark admitted.

With the raincoat buttoned to his chin to conceal his evening clothes he left the Commodore, stopped at a lunch counter in Grand Central and had coffee and toast. There were more people in the station now, a steady stream of early commuters coming from the various tracks.

He went out onto Vanderbilt Avenue. The city was growing noisier and more crowded. The streetlights were out, daylight filtered palely into the canyons. There were more taxis and trucks and buses. Stores were being unlocked, windows uncovered, merchandise set on display. People were beginning to crowd the streets on their way to work.

Mark walked through the throng unnoticed—or so he hoped—but watchful. However absorbed he might be in his thoughts, he had long ago trained himself to be constantly alert for trouble.

It's a wonderful city, he thought. Here almost every activity known to man is going on. People are finding ways to make life better, easier, more productive. Opening up new horizons. Painting pictures and composing music and writing books. Exploring new fields of science and technology, new ways of relieving pain and preventing disease.

It's a terrible city. Somewhere at this moment someone may be killing someone else or planning to. Someone is committing a robbery or any one of a thousand crimes. Youngsters are starting on the path that diverges from good citizenship by stealing cars and television sets for easy cash.

And yet we can make this city what we want it to be, wonderful or terrible. Like it or not, we build a city in our own image.

On Gramercy Park he unlocked the door of one of the few private houses left on that enchanting old square, tossed his raincoat on a carved bench, climbed wearily up to his bedroom on the second floor. Before undressing he stood for a long time looking out of the window, watching day awaken the city. The square itself still slept.

In the Sobelli town house, Julie Bryce would be asleep. Julie! He had told the government men the truth. He had no right to love because there was no guarantee he could make to a woman that he could live a safe and normal life. He had arrived at that decision for himself, without outside pressure. But he hadn't expected to meet anyone like Julie. The great eyes like brown velvet, the warm curve of her lips, the candor and honesty that were implicit in her nature. She had represented all the dreams he had had as a boy. She was better than the dreams. But there was no place in his life for dreams. If life were to be made safe for other people, his own had to be unsafe.

All his self-control had been required to keep away from Julie on the ship. True, he had weakened and asked her to dance with him. He had stood beside her on the deck and seen the moon reflected in her eyes, seen their expression when she looked at him, as though something had leaped between them, a sudden sympathy, an understanding without words.

I can't let it happen, he told himself. I was a fool to dance with her again tonight. Not that her peace of mind will be cut up like mine. Still I'm glad she didn't witness that incident when Lisa Maydock hurled herself into my arms. If she remembers me at all, I don't want it to be shabbily.

No one must hurt Julie. Nothing must hurt her. I love her, he told himself. I gave myself away tonight to my colleagues but I don't care. I love her. And I know, somehow I know, that I could make her love me.

Stop it, Sefton! he warned himself angrily. You have a job to do. A big job.

He undressed and went to bed but not to sleep. He had always supposed that love would be a delightful sensation. He had not dreamed that it could cause so much pain. He stared at the ceiling, hating his job, rebelling at the thought that he must let the girl go. For her own sake, he told himself. For her own sake.

Then he sat up in bed. No decision had been made that night about protecting Julie. He would have to arrange something himself. As soon as the Princess was likely to be awake he would call her, make her see that the situation was urgent. Dangerous.

And he slept at last, dreaming that he was on horseback, galloping across the prairie. There was wind in his hair and the bitter scent of sagebrush in his nostrils and a jagged line of incredible mountains shutting out the horizon on the west. On the east there was unlimited space. And beside him, laughing, rode Julie. They galloped on and on into the engulfing darkness of sleep.

IX

After a few hours' restless sleep Mark was at his telephone by ten o'clock. The butler at the Sobelli house regretted that Her Highness had left strict orders that she was not to be disturbed. Could he take a message? There was no message, Mark said. Might Perkins know who was calling? It didn't matter. He would call later. Oh, by the way, did Perkins happen to know whether Miss Bryce was still sleeping?

Miss Bryce, Perkins said, had gone out. Mark gripped the telephone uneasily. No guard had been arranged for her. Heaven knew where the girl was or what might be happening. One thing might be relied upon. The dope ring would not let any time escape if they believed Julie represented a danger to them.

"You don't happen to know when Miss Bryce will return?" Mark asked.

"I believe she planned to go riding in Central Park, sir. She was dressed in riding clothes."

"Thank you."

Mark put down the telephone, dressed in riding clothes, and rang the stables to arrange for a horse. At the same time he asked casually, "By the way, has Miss Bryce called yet?"

"Oh, yes, sir. We've just sent a man with a horse to meet her at the opening to that bridle path—you know the one?" He described it.

"Have a man meet me there," Mark said. "The name is Sefton. Give me a good mount. Last time it might as well have been used for trucking."

"We'll do our best, sir, but this is no racing stable, and we don't run to thoroughbreds. Most of our riders wouldn't be safe on them."

With a feeling of panic Mark ran down the stairs, brushed aside his servant who was setting a table for his breakfast, shouted that he would be back to change, probably in a couple of hours, and went out to hail a taxi.

They are never easy to find around Gramercy Park, that old-world cul-de-sac in the heart of Manhattan, and Mark had to go around the park to the hotel on the north side before he could signal an empty cab.

Even with the extra speed that is now made possible by one-way traffic, it seemed to him that no trip had ever been made so slowly. Not more than a snail's pace. He found himself sitting on the edge of his seat as though he could increase the speed of the taxi, and forced himself, as a matter of discipline and self-control, to sit back and relax.

A man was waiting with a saddled horse when Mark came up. For a moment Mark's knowledge of horses took precedence over his anxiety as he looked over the mount he had hired. He wasn't overly enthusiastic.

"Well, of course, sir," the groom said, "they take a beating from amateurs. Most people who rent horses don't know a thing about riding. A really fine horse would be worthless in no time. We have some good sturdy hacks that will stand up to a lot of punishment. That's all we can claim."

"How about Miss Bryce? Do you have any idea where I'll find her?"

The man shook his head. "Miss Bryce rides our horses quite often. She usually goes that way," and he gestured with a big hand, deftly pocketed Mark's tip, and watched with approval the light way in which Mark mounted. For once a horse was in the hands of a man who knew how to ride and he need not worry.

Mark, accustomed to a western saddle, never really enjoyed English saddles but he rode well, relaxed, man and horse moving as one.

Now that he knew Julie was just ahead of him, that he was bound to encounter her before long, his uneasiness disappeared. He grinned rather guiltily to himself. When he had learned where she was, it had been unnecessary to follow her. Nothing could happen to her on a bridle path in Central Park. This trip had been an act of pure self-indulgence. He had wanted to see her again. He was going to see her. Any minute now.

The sun was hot, as it often is in early September, and the air was cool, with a bracing crispness that foretold of autumn. The windows in apartment buildings on Central Park West gleamed gold with the morning sun. There was a surprising crowd in the park. Young mothers gossiped on benches, their babies in carriages in front of them, enjoying the sunlight and fresh air that were not obtainable in their small apartments. Elderly men, their years of retirement stretching long and empty, strolled along the paths, hands clasped behind their backs, or fed the ubiquitous squirrels. A young couple lay on the ground, arms around each other, blissfully unaware of anything but themselves. An open carriage went past containing a young couple who appeared to be honeymooners. Around a pool small boys squatted, pushing tiny boats out into the water. A balloon man was doing a fairly lively business.

Ahead there was the sound of hoofs on the bridle path and Mark urged his own mount into a canter, then checked when he saw that the riders were an unknown couple. The girl was apparently out for her first horseback ride, clinging madly to the horse's mane. The man accompanying her was obviously from the stable. He saw Mark's grin of commiseration and winked at him.

"Now, miss," he said, apparently repeating something he had been saying over and over, "we're only at a walk. You can't fall off. Just relax."

There was no one in sight now but a young woman, sitting on a bench, absorbed in a book while her small charge ran, eyes up, following the course of a balloon he was holding. In a sudden gust of wind the balloon escaped his hand and startled a horse, making it rear. Then the little boy ran onto the bridle path in pursuit of the lost toy and in front of the careening horse.

Mark saw the slim girl try to pull up her mount as it danced out of control in a kind of circle. He leaped to the ground, flung down the reins, caught up the screaming child in a few long strides and turned to restore it to the now thoroughly aroused and frenzied mother, who was running toward him, screaming.

Julie's plunging horse was now out of control and tearing along the bridle path. Mark handed the boy to his mother, leaped on his own horse, and sent his mount thundering after Julie's.

She was in sight around the next curve and he was gaining on her. Then, and he thanked God for the better horse and for his better riding, he was abreast. He leaned far out, seized the bridle of the runaway horse, crowded it to the side of the path, brought it to a halt.

For a moment Julie sat slumping in the saddle and then she turned, white-faced, to look at her rescuer. Her eyes seemed impossibly large as they widened in astonished recognition.

"You," she whispered.

He lifted her out of the saddle, onto the ground. Just for one uncontrollable moment his arms tightened and he held her crushed against him so that she felt the pounding of his heart.

"Oh God," he whispered. "I was so afraid for you."

Then his arms dropped and he stood back, half expecting her to be angry. It seemed to him that her eyes were smiling as they looked at him, that lovely color had rushed into the cheeks that had been so white, that she swayed toward him slightly.

Then the lovely warm welcome in her face was gone, shadowed by some thought he could not follow. She held out her hand. Her voice was cool as she said, "I can't begin to tell you how grateful I am, Mr. Sefton." She gasped and her voice sharpened. "Oh, the little boy! Is he—"

"Quite all right. I hope, for his sake, his mother manages to keep an eye on him next time he plays near the bridle path. That must have been a very engrossing book she was reading." He took the reins of both horses. "Look here, I'll have to return these to the stable. We can't very well go anywhere in riding clothes and I'd like to talk to you. Would you mind—that is, will you wait for me here? I shan't be long. It's a wonderful day for a walk."

There was a conflict warring in Julie's face. She kept

seeing Lady Maydock in Mark's arms, hearing her voice as she spoke to him, hearing the warning she had given the girl herself. When she smiled at last it was without her usual warmth.

"Of course I'll wait. Actually I am most grateful to you for taking charge of this horse. I never want to see him again. Anyhow, aren't you supposed to owe something to the person who saves your life?"

"I won't hold you to that, Miss Bryce," Mark said in his deep, grave voice. "I have no taste for unwilling victims."

Then he mounted his own horse and cantered down the bridle path and back to the stables, leading Julie's mount. Julie was left, her eyes followed him. How beautifully he rode. How swiftly he reacted. One moment she had been in terror for the small boy who had rushed into the path of her horse, the next moment she had been in terror for herself when she realized her mount was out of control. And Mark had come; Mark had stopped the runaway; Mark had saved the little boy and lifted her to the ground and held her—for one ecstatic moment—held her as though he would never let her go, his voice husky with his fear for her.

She sat on a bench in the sun, feet in their polished riding boots, beautifully tailored riding breeches and well-fitting jacket. She was aware of white tufts of cloud drifting idly across the blue of the sky. She was so deep in thought that time passed almost unnoticed until she heard the sound of running feet. Mark was returning. When he caught sight of her he slowed to a walk.

For a moment Julie exulted. *He was running to meet me*, she thought. Then she watched him, her expression bland, unrevealing.

He held out his hand. "Shall we walk for a while?" She let him draw her to her feet, their hands clung for a moment, and then they were walking sedately side by side.

"How on earth did you learn how to manage a horse that way?" Julie asked, when they had walked for several minutes in silence.

"I could ride almost as soon as I could walk," he explained. "I have a ranch in Montana. My best dreams have always centered around living there and breeding horses. Living there even if I have to turn the place into a dude ranch to make it pay."

"But why don't you?" she asked.

"There are things that seem more important than simply following one's heart's desire," Mark told her.

"What kind of things?"

He hesitated and then sidetracked her question by telling her about his childhood in the West.

"Not the Wild West of the movies," he assured her. "Actually, with the exception of a few short years in a few tiny towns, it never was that kind of Wild West. The real story is much better than the movies. I wish you could know my country. The air is clean and clear and you can see for miles, except to the west where the great mountains rise. There aren't many big trees except for cottonwoods. There isn't always enough water, but there is space and elbowroom and a kind of freedom and human dignity I've never found anywhere else."

He laughed at his own enthusiasm.

"It sounds like Utopia," Julie commented, with a shy look at him. When he was interested, as he was now, his face lost its grimness. It seemed younger.

"To most people," Mark told her, "Utopia represents a situation in which people lie around and don't do much of anything and just enjoy the fat of the land without earning it. That isn't true of a working ranch. There is hard, grueling labor, long hours and lonely nights of herding cattle and tough struggles with deep snow and the hazards of drought and blizzard, of disease and rattlesnakes, of all the incalculable factors that can nullify a man's work through no fault of his own."

"But you love it."

"I love it."

"What brought you east?"

They had reached the reservoir and started to walk around the famous mile where so many people over the years have paced in search of health or exercise or an escape from their immediate problems. A couple of determined joggers lumbered past and then they were alone.

"College first. Princeton. Then war service. Then—"
Mark came to an abrupt stop.

Julie smiled at him. "Is that the end of the story?"

"Enough for this installment. It's your turn now."

"Age twenty-three," Julie told him obediently. "Health
good. Education Smith. Parents both dead in an influen-
za epidemic. Aunt Georgia has taken their place, given
me everything I have. Everything. I can't remember her
ever refusing me anything except—"

"Except?" Mark prompted her.

"She wanted me to do the usual things, make my
debut, follow a standard social pattern of parties and
shopping and all that. I didn't want to. Not when she
works so hard. I've always wanted to go into the business but she flatly refuses. She says—"

"Well?"

"She says I'm an all-or-nothing person and that I'll be
bound to marry soon and I won't want to be involved in
business responsibilities."

"And are you?"

"Am I what?" she asked.

"Going to marry soon?"

"I—don't know."

"Your aunt is right, you know," Mark told her. "Right,
at least, about not going into the business. Stay away
from it. In fact, I wish you would stay away from New
York. Go somewhere. Go anywhere. Take a cruise."

Julie's heart sank. He wanted her to go away! Anywhere, apparently, so long as she went. Did he dislike
her that much? Or—what was wrong, anyhow? That was
what Bert had said. Get a job or go away.

She stopped short, forcing Mark to stop too. She faced
him squarely.

"Mr. Sefton, why is my aunt afraid of you?"

She could read nothing but complete astonishment in
his face. "What on earth—?" he began, bewildered. "My
dear Miss Bryce, I can assure you that the Princess is not
afraid of me. There is no conceivable reason why she
should be. What made you think anything so preposterous?"

"You see, I happened to come back to New York from
Westchester while you were at the house," Julie said.

"That was the day in June after the house had been robbed and Aunt Georgia's jewelry had been stolen. I heard you and my aunt talking." There was a moment while she remembered running across her bedroom to catch a glimpse of the man with the deep voice, and Mark wondered what reason there was for the color that suddenly flooded her cheeks. "I asked her who you were and she said you were an insurance investigator."

She looked up quickly but there was no expression on Mark's face. It was completely unrevealing.

"The second officer on the ship—"

Mark grinned at her in amusement. "The one who fell so madly in love with you?"

"The one who—oh, no, but he was very nice—he said you had been a passenger several times before and you were not an insurance investigator."

Still Mark made no comment.

"And last night—this morning—neither my aunt nor I could sleep. Perhaps we were too tired. Anyhow, I was talking in her sitting room and asked why she had pretended not to know you when I introduced you last night. I said I knew you had been in the house. And she said I was never, never to speak of that again. Not to anyone."

Mark walked on at her side, his face set. At length he said, "I can only repeat what I told you before, because it is the truth. Your aunt is not afraid of me."

"But she is afraid of someone, of something. She said so. Horribly afraid. Mr. Sefton, what are you and my aunt doing?"

"I can't tell you," he said at last.

"Are you an insurance investigator?"

He hesitated, made up his mind. "I am not."

"What are you?"

"I can't tell you that, either."

"But it is dangerous, isn't it?"

"It could be," Mark admitted. "That is why I wish to God, Julie, that you would go away. You can do no good by becoming involved. You could do great harm, not only to yourself but to something else, something more important than you are."

Neither of them seemed to be conscious of his use of

her first name. At last he took her arm, turned her to face him. "Will you go away?"

She shook her head. "You mean run away. No, I won't."

"I'll do my best to keep an eye on you, but it may not always be possible. At least, it won't be for very long. A few weeks, at most."

"Why should you keep an eye on me?"

"Someone has to." He laughed shortly. "It's odd that it should have to be me because the funny thing is that I've done everything possible to stay away from you."

"Why?" she asked imprudently.

There was a smile in his eyes. "You know why, Julie."

There was no answering smile in the great dark eyes that surveyed him gravely. "You mean because of Lady Maydock?"

His lips tightened. "Keep away from that woman, Julie."

She laughed. "She warned me about you, too."

"Did you believe her?" he asked, and his eyes forced her to reply honestly.

"Not her words. But I believed my own eyes."

"Oh." He expelled a long breath. "So you did see that. I hoped you hadn't. Sometimes there is nothing so unreliable as the evidence of your eyes. What you saw last night was misleading, and intended to be misleading." He paused, scrawled something on a page in a notebook, ripped it out and gave it to her. "This is a way of reaching me."

"Thank you, I won't—"

He put the paper in her hand, closed her fingers over it. "Keep it. Please, Julie. Someday you may need me. Please."

She looked pointedly at the hand that had closed so firmly over hers and he dropped it. After a moment's hesitation she put the paper in a pocket of her riding jacket. She glanced at her wristwatch. "I must be getting back to the house."

Without protest he led her toward Fifth Avenue and hailed a taxi. He helped her in but made no attempt to follow her, closing the door behind her. His hand went up in a slight gesture of farewell and he turned away.

Impulsively she leaned forward. "Mr. Sefton!" She raised her voice. "Mark! Thank you. I haven't forgotten that you saved my life this morning. Thank you, Mark."

He returned her wave before he stepped back to signal a second cab into which he climbed.

Julie gave her driver the address of her aunt's house and sat back in the seat, going over her interview with Mark Sefton. Her fingers groped in the pocket of her jacket for a sheet of paper. There was an address on Gramercy Park, a Gramercy telephone number, and a second, unidentified telephone number. Below, he had scrawled: "One of these will reach me within minutes, if you ever need help. But be careful. Your Mark."

Your Mark. But he had said she would interfere with something more important than she was. He had tried to keep away from her and he said that she knew why. But if he loved her why—why—

The driver said wearily, "This is the number you gave me, lady," and Julie sat up with a start to find they were in front of her aunt's house. As she stepped out of the taxi she came face to face with Charles Norton.

For a moment he seemed startled, then he smiled. "Miss Bryce! I told you that we would be meeting soon." He signaled for her taxi to wait for him.

X

The butler was mistaken. Princess Sobelli was not asleep. After Julie had left her, she had gone to her beautiful bedroom but not to sleep. She piled pillows high behind her and reached for a book on the table beside her bed. It was a book by Catherine Drinker Bowen on the writing of biography but, delightful as the writing was, the restless reader let the book fall from her hand.

How could anyone write the life of another? What did anyone know of another? The outward actions? But sometimes these had little or nothing to do with the real person.

The evidence of people who had known the subject of the biography? But how much did any person know of any other? How much did even her closest friends know of her?

She thought of Brooks Mansfield, who loved her and believed in her. She did not know what he saw in her but one thing she felt certain of: he would be appalled if he were ever to know, upright and fine as he was, what she was doing. He would find the whole thing not only dangerous, as of course it was, but shady, dishonest, inexcusable. And Georgia Sobelli, looking honestly at herself, realized all of a sudden that she could not bear to have him see her that way. She wanted his love and his regard and, above all, his respect. There were moments, moments that came increasingly often, when she longed to discard her title, to sell out her business, to marry Brooks and let him take care of her.

I get so tired, so tired, she murmured to herself. So alone.

She pulled out the extra pillows, tossed them on the

carpet, and tried to settle down to sleep, but her eyes were wide open in the darkness. So alone, she repeated. But I made a promise to myself, a solemn promise, that I would carry this thing through. That unfinished business. For Dino.

She repeated the words "For Dino." Then she realized, with a kind of shock, that the words were no longer true. For Dino—yes, in the beginning. That was true enough. But now she was sticking to her perilous course for something bigger than her love for Dino. In fact—

In fact, she was aware, in the years since his death, her memory of Dino had grown less sharp—in some ways, almost hazy. She had loved him deeply. Adored him. He had been Romeo and Prince Florizel rolled into one. The most handsome man she had ever seen. An engaging manner. A delightful smile. And he had loved her. Loved her truly. But even at the peak of her infatuation there had been moments when she had been aware of the weakness of his mouth, for all its delightful smile, and she had been alarmed. Charming as he was, loving as a husband, there was no real strength in the man.

There had been years of happiness that seemed, at least in retrospect, to be all sunlight. Then had come Dino's illness. It had not been a serious illness but it had been accompanied by considerable pain. And the incompetent though well-meaning doctor from a small village near their summer villa had prescribed morphine for relief of the pain.

If she had only been there to realize what was happening, Georgia Sobelli thought—but there was no use in *if*. The harm had been done by the time she returned from a few weeks with an old friend in Switzerland. At first she had not noticed the difference. Then she began to see how her husband's whole personality changed with time; there had been days when his eyes were dull and he seemed lethargic, so that she believed the illness had returned. And he began to do foolish, irresponsible things. Within the space of three years he had dissipated his fortune, leaving nothing but the huge palace and no money to maintain it. And then one morning he had not awakened. He had taken an overdose of morphine. Only then did she realize that her beloved husband had become a drug addict.

To help her recover from the shock of her loss, she plunged into work and developed the Sobelli cosmetics firm, using the snob appeal of the title to assist her in becoming established. She discovered, in surprise, that she was a sound businesswoman.

But always, in the back of her mind, was her resentment at the ineptitude of the man who had started her husband on the drug habit and her loathing for the unscrupulous criminals who, later on, had catered to it. She would, she thought, gladly and without hesitation, sacrifice anything, even her own life, to fight what seemed to her one of the world's great evils.

So when Mark Sefton had approached her, months before, she had listened to his plan. He had showed her his credentials, explained that his job was tracking down narcotics rings, and told her of his idea.

"What is happening, Princess, is that new ways are constantly found to smuggle in dope. We often find the cache, but although we sometimes catch the small fry, the distributors, we rarely lay hands on the men at the top. What we need is to be able to follow a transaction from beginning to end. Then we can get the people higher up and see that they receive such long prison sentences and such enormous fines that we'll strip the profit out of the business. And without profit there will be no business. People don't take such risks for nothing."

He had, she realized now in some amusement, been as surprised as he was relieved by the interest she had displayed and her willingness to cooperate. She had not, in loyalty to Dino's memory, explained why she would take any risk to help fight the dope racket.

"What do you have in mind, Mr. Sefton? I assume you feel I can be of help."

He hesitated, studying her. "First, I would need your absolute assurance that, whether you go ahead with this or not, you will discuss it with no other human being. A lot depends on that."

She did not hesitate at all. "That you may be quite sure of."

"Second, I cannot go farther without telling you that the narcotics racket is headed by completely unscrupulous people who can call upon addicts who will do anything to obtain the drug, to obey their orders. Sometimes unpleasant orders. In other words, this is a dangerous undertaking."

She nodded thoughtfully, her beautiful face without expression. "That is fair enough. I think it's worth the risk."

"Third, you have built a highly successful business. What we have in mind may imperil its reputation, lower the value of your stock, all that. At least temporarily. Until—and unless—we can pull this off. If we are successful in what we are attempting to do, you will be completely cleared and your actions as a fine citizen publicly acknowledged. But I cannot guarantee success, Princess. And I cannot, in honesty, overestimate the extent of the risk you will run."

There had been a long silence. Georgia Sobelli thought of her position in the eyes of the world, she thought of her luxurious life, she thought of the business she had built, at what a cost no one would ever know, and of the staff of employees not only in New York, but in at least three other countries, whose welfare depended on the business. And then she thought of Dino, his brilliant eyes dulled, his mouth slack, his life, like his palace, in ruins.

"I will do it, Mr. Sefton."

For a moment they exchanged a measuring look and then he held out his hand. "I thank you, Princess. So will the whole department. Now then—" He explained the plan he had conceived, while she listened, nodding to indicate her comprehension. When he had finished, there was a long silence.

"I understand your plan," she said, "and I believe it has a good chance of working. Certainly I could do my part. But what I do not understand is how this will enable you to achieve your real objective: that is, to get hold of the heads of the conspiracy."

He explained.

ii

After her sleepless night following the Maskers Ball Princess Sobelli finally rang her bell for breakfast. While the maid was adjusting the tray she asked, "Is Miss Bryce still asleep?"

"No, Your Highness, she had breakfast a little after nine and has already gone out."

"Gone out!" The Princess wondered at the resilience of youth. At five in the morning Julie had been exhausted, but in a few hours she had enough energy to start out again. I must be getting old, the Princess told herself with a wry smile.

"She left word for Your Highness that she planned to ride in Central Park and that she would not be gone very long."

When the Princess had bathed in her famous sunken tub and worked on her tired face, she had Simone massage the tense muscles at the back of her neck before doing her hair and slipping over her head a black and white print dress. For a moment she thought regretfully of her pearl earrings and then shrugged off the regret. There were more important things.

She was adjusting a small white hat when Simone came back from the door to say, "A gentleman called a little while ago and asked for you. When he was told you were asleep he said he would call later. He left no name. Then he asked for Miss Bryce. Perkins said she was going to ride in Central Park."

The Princess felt a momentary pang of uneasiness and then she shrugged it off. Not important, she decided, though it was odd the man had not left his name.

"And a gentleman has just arrived. Perkins put him in the drawing room."

The Princess arched astonished eyebrows. "Without inquiring to find out whether I was at home?"

"He said he was an old friend of His Highness and that he knows you well, too. He said he had an appointment." The maid looked at the Princess's startled face and away again. One hand was clenched.

"Who is he?"

The maid held out a small silver tray on which there was a card. Without picking it up, the Princess read, "Mr. Charles Fairbanks Norton."

She looked at it, the maid thought, as though it were a rattlesnake coiled to strike. Then she said, "I will see him at once."

She gathered up the white gloves and handbag the maid handed her. Somewhat to the latter's surprise, she went down in the elevator. Simone would have been even more surprised to know that her employer's knees were shaking so that she dared not attempt to walk down the stairs.

There was no indication of this when she strolled into the drawing room. Charles Norton got up quickly from the big carved chair by the fireplace, crushing out his cigarette.

"Good morning," she said. "There seems to be some misunderstanding. Perkins tells me that you claim to have an appointment with me." She stressed the word *claim*.

"I think it is time we have a little talk, Princess, and come to an understanding." There was an undercurrent of insolence in his manner.

"I am about to leave." She remained standing. "If you can tell me in the next ten minutes I can listen. After that, I have other demands on my time."

He admired the picture she made, still beautiful and graceful and exquisitely groomed, her manner impeccable, her clothing in perfect taste, her air chilly. In spite of himself, he stirred awkwardly. Then he remembered that she was too deep in the thing to get out.

"I guess you can take some time," he said, and the insolence in his manner was more pronounced.

For a moment she stood jerking her long gloves through her hand and then she sat down, deliberately choosing the big carved chair he had vacated, so that he had to take a smaller one. A minor victory, perhaps, but it put her, in a sense, at the head of the table.

She glanced at her watch. "Well, Mr. Norton?"

"Very well, indeed," he told her.

"I was greatly surprised last night when you made

yourself known to me in that public manner. I had understood clearly that we were not, in any circumstances, to meet. Certainly not in such a fashion."

He grinned impudently. "But, after all, I'm a great friend of your dead husband, and dear Dino—"

"Never speak of him like that again! Do you understand?" Anger lashed at him as though she had used a whip, and he was startled at the storm he had aroused. You never knew. A woman would go along meekly enough, accept your conditions, agree to anything you said. Then all of a sudden—bingo! She blew wide open. In that mood she would be just crazy enough to give up the whole thing.

"Well—sorry, and all that. But it seemed like an easy way to establish a social connection."

"There can be no conceivable reason for any social connection between us."

He flushed at her tone. "You'd like at least to have a report on progress, wouldn't you?" He was slouching in his chair, one knee crossed over the other. He lighted a cigarette and the scent of Turkish tobacco was heavy in the air. He had not asked her permission to smoke.

Princess Sobelli touched a bell and when Perkins appeared she said, "Turn on the air-conditioning, please." She waved a hand idly to disperse the smoke.

Again Norton found himself flushing. Confound the woman! Trying to put him in his place, was she? They'd find out who was the master here. Acting as though she owned the earth and here she was, her business on the rocks, pulling a fake theft of her own jewelry to cash in on the insurance, and agreeing to all his suggestions. High-hat him, would she?

"We've got things rolling," he said, trying to swallow his anger. He was no match for her when it came to words, to social snubs. But she would find that he was a match for her at the game she was trying to play. "The stuff came in safely from Cairo. I've got it packed away in closets in the palace. That's the reason I had to see you at once. Get off a cable to Giuseppe and send him away. I don't care what pretext you use, but we want the place to be clear while the stuff is being put into the perfume bottles. Our people will be ready to move in day after tomorrow."

Georgia Sobelli nodded.

"We figure on making shipment within ten days. The compacts from England and lipsticks from Paris should move at the same time. So we'll have to put our own man in your shipping department. We had better do that at once. Say that you need extra people for unloading the stuff and we'll provide the man. He'll have to work nights, of course."

Again the Princess nodded her comprehension.

"The day we move the stuff out of your shipping department, with our own labels on it, headed for our distributors, you'll get paid."

There was a faint flush on the woman's cheeks but she simply nodded again.

"Good." He crushed out the cigarette and for a moment she hoped that he was leaving. Instead, he settled back in his chair. He had a hard face, she thought. There was no imagination in it but he had a quick intelligence and he was a born plotter. He was not a man who really liked taking chances. He could be ruthless. He could also, she suspected, be frightened. She did not want him frightened now; she preferred to be the one who seemed to be easily terrorized and dominated.

"So far, Princess," he said abruptly, and the voice which had been pleasant had somehow coarsened, "you've been okay. No trouble at all." He looked at her, his eyes narrowing. "A real good girl."

She slid her hands behind her back because they betrayed her, her fingers clawing at the fabric of the upholstery.

"But we've got to keep it like that, haven't we?"

This time he waited. After a moment she said, "I don't understand. What do you mean?"

"The little niece," Norton said. "Julie Bryce." He leaned forward, his chin jutting, eyes glaring. "What was Julie Bryce doing in the Sobelli palace, Princess?"

She took the blow without so much as a flicker of an eyelash, her face as beautifully cold and remote as ever. "My niece had never seen the palace. I had told her that the place was simply falling apart, that there was nothing to see, but she was curious."

"She just happened to go to the palace the day I made the delivery?"

"Julie knows absolutely nothing about this business, Mr. Norton. Nothing at all. She is completely in the clear."

"Yeah?"

There was a hint of desperation in the Princess's voice now. "I—swear to you." Her voice broke. "Julie is innocent. She was just curious. That's all. Just curious. Surely you believe me! If she had told me what she intended, I would have prevented it in some way. It was only an impulse on her part. A natural curiosity about a place of which she had heard so much. The strange thing would have been if she had not been interested in seeing it when she was in Florence. And to Americans palaces still carry an aura of glamour, you know, even when they are little more than ruins."

"Curiosity," Norton said, his voice almost a snarl. The Princess searched his face but found no clue to tell her what he was thinking. He got up. He was leaving at last. He turned back from the door. "Just remember, Princess, the old saying: Curiosity killed the cat."

When he had gone, Georgia Sobelli sank back in her chair, covering her face with her hands. She had said, and said voluntarily, that she would do anything to help end this hideous narcotics traffic. But she had not meant to include Julie. Julie must not be hurt. Must not. In one way or another she must find a way to get Julie out of the city, out of the range of the dope ring, out of danger.

XI

Curiosity killed the cat. Georgia Sobelli sank down on a chair in the great drawing room. From the beginning she had known of the desperate chances she was taking. But they were for herself. Not Julie. Never Julie! Now Charles Norton had made himself clear. If he were to believe that she had lied about her niece, that Julie had any reason for going to the palace beyond the simple curiosity she had indicated, the girl would be in danger. Horrible danger.

She held her head between her hands, rocking from side to side. There must be some way of saving Julie. There had to be.

Perkins was pacing through the long hallway with his usual deliberate step, and pride made her sit erect and brace herself for what might be coming. The outside door opened, there was a murmur of voices, and then Julie appeared in riding clothes. Her boots, usually highly polished, looked scuffed and dusty.

"Good morning, Aunt Georgia! Awake at last. And you've already had a caller, I see."

Georgia Sobelli dropped her gloves and took her time in picking them up. "And how do you know that?"

"I met Mr. Norton. He was just leaving when I got out of the taxi."

Her aunt made no comment and Julie noticed the white line around her lips, the strain around her eyes.

"Has Mr. Norton anything to do with the danger you may be in, Aunt Georgia?"

The Princess was in full control again. "My dear, I do not want to discuss all that business. If I hadn't been so tired and upset last night, I'd never have mentioned it. Now I don't want you to refer to it again."

"But, Aunt Georgia," Julie came to put her arms around the older woman, "you've done so much for me. Can't I share this?"

"No!" It was almost a cry. "Julie, I want you to go away from here. Go up to the Westchester house for a few weeks. Or, better still, take a cruise."

That was what Mark Sefton had said. Go away. Go away.

"But I was looking forward to helping in the transformation of May Williams," Julie said, trying to speak gaily. "And anyhow, I can't go anywhere until I have a shampoo and manicure."

"Arrange your own time at the shop," her aunt said absently. Then her voice deepened. "Julie—after that, will you go if I—if I beg you?"

There was a long painful silence, and then Julie said, "I don't mean to be stubborn, but somehow I feel that I have to stay."

"What am I to do!" The Princess was half laughing, half crying. "I can't lock you up." She started toward the door, holding the handbag and gloves. "At least—keep away from that man Norton, Julie."

"That suits me," Julie replied. "I don't like him one single bit."

Perkins came in. "Mr. Mansfield is calling." At the Princess's nod he plugged in a telephone and handed it to her.

"Brooks? ... The Royal Ballet doing *Romeo and Juliet*? I'd love it. ... Why don't you dine here? ... The Pierre? ... Seven o'clock." The glowing smile on her face faded when she had set down the telephone. She looked at Julie, a frown between her brows, a curious alarm in her voice. "But what will you do tonight? Do you have a date?"

"As I had only three hours' sleep and nearly got myself killed this morning, I'm going to bed right after dinner."

"Killed!" The word was almost a scream.

"I'm so sorry, Aunt Georgia! I didn't mean to startle you."

Her aunt gave an impatient laugh. "Startle me! Good

heavens! What really happened? I thought you went riding." She looked in perplexity at the riding clothes.

"I did, but my horse was startled by a balloon that escaped from a little boy. Then the child ran almost in front of my horse to retrieve it and the horse was frightened and ran away, out of control. I was nearly thrown off, but Mr. Sefton happened to be riding and he caught my horse by the bridle. So after he had returned the horses to the stable, we walked for a while and then I came home."

It had not seemed to Julie that her aunt could get any paler. "Mr. Sefton—just happened to go riding this morning?"

"Why not?" Julie was puzzled.

Her aunt remembered the telephone call from a man who had not given his name, a man to whom Perkins had said that Julie was riding in the park. She summoned up a stiff smile. "That was—very fortunate for you. Well, I have a busy day." She turned back from the door. "Julie, won't you please reconsider and go up to the Westchester house for a few weeks?"

Julie shook her head, soft hair brushing against her cheeks as she did so.

With a little gesture of despair and defeat her aunt went out of the room. A few minutes later Julie saw her walking swiftly down the street—walking was good for her figure—a beautiful, infinitely smart woman who seemed to be on top of the world.

The Princess walked fast, but not fast enough to move ahead of her swirling thoughts. One thing seemed to be crystal clear. Mark Sefton had telephoned that morning to know where Julie was; he had not been in the park on horseback by sheer coincidence. *Mark Sefton knew about Julie's danger.* But whether she was relieved at the knowledge that there was someone to share her anxiety about Julie and protect her or whether she was more frightened by this evidence that Norton had been telling the truth about the danger, she did not know.

She walked on, unaware of the eyes that recognized and followed her. "Princess Sobelli ... the one with the cosmetics business. Even more beautiful than her pictures, isn't she, because they don't do justice to her coloring ... a title and a fortune and beauty. Nothing in the world to worry about. Some people have everything."

ii

Not until the interval did Georgia Sobelli tear her eyes from the stage. "Would you have believed it possible," she asked, "to see a Shakespeare play, complete in all its beauty and drama, without words? Somehow the words are all implicit in the dancing. I think it is the loveliest ballet I've even seen. Lovelier than *Giselle* even, in some ways. It has everything: the dancing, the music, those lovely muted autumn colors. And—always— the beauty."

Brooks Mansfield, who had slept a great part of the day and seemed completely refreshed from the night at the Maskers Ball, was watching her covertly. In spite of the careful but discreet makeup he could detect signs of strain and fatigue in the face he knew and loved so well. It was almost haggard.

"What a terrible pity," she went on, "for artists today to rebel against beauty. It's like rebelling against life itself. But I suppose, in a way, that is just what they are doing. In the past artists were on the side of life, enriching and ennobling it. Now they protest against it. But we still have things like this; evenings of pure beauty that transcend all the petty things, or at least give us the strength and courage to tackle them."

"I hoped you would like it, Georgia. When I first saw it done in Rome I thought that I would like to share it with you. Few people have your—well, it's a fresh, almost childlike, response to beauty. But that's only fair, of course."

"Why?"

"Because you have so much beauty to give that you should get some in return."

There was nothing cold in her face now. It glowed with warmth. "You pay such lovely compliments, Brooks."

"I never compliment you. It isn't a compliment to say

that you are beautiful. You must know that. Everyone has told you so for years. One of the famous beauties of your day."

She laughed at him. "At my age? After a sleepless night? My dear, don't be absurd."

Somewhat to her surprise he asked quickly, "A sleepless night?" He went on before she could answer, "Georgia, are you in trouble?"

She made no answer. There was a momentary flash from the diamond bracelet clasped on her wrist as her hand jerked, and then she was motionless.

When he realized that she was not going to reply he went on, his voice so low that no one else could hear him, though their box was empty except for themselves, the other occupants having gone out in search of refreshments or acquaintances or a cigarette.

"If you are in trouble, I will help you, Georgia. It does not matter what it is. You can rely on me. Whatever you are doing—and I've guessed for some time that you are up to something—I will back you."

"Brooks!" There were tears in her eyes when she turned to look at him.

"I love you, Georgia. I've loved you for ten years, since the first time I met you at a White House reception. There was an awful crush but you seemed to be the only person in the place."

He went on quickly, before she could summon up a way of stopping him. "You have been faithful all this time to the memory of Dino Sobelli. I can understand that. He was your first love, your dearest love. I don't ask for anything like that. But can't you learn to care for me a little? You and I are both alone. We could make a full life together instead of two empty ones apart."

"Oh, Brooks!" she whispered. "If you only knew!"

"I want to know. I want to share things with you. But even if I can't, even if you won't let me share, I'd settle for what you are willing to give me."

She was looking steadily at him now, her glorious eyes brilliant with unshed tears. "That full life—I wish I could believe in it, Brooks."

"Why can't you?"

"I can't explain." As he started to protest she touched

his arm with her fingers. "No, that is true. I am pledged
to a certain course of action and I can't—I wouldn't if I
could—turn back."

"How long is this to go on?" he asked.

"A month—at the longest. By that time I'll be able to
tell you the truth, the whole truth, and nothing but the
truth."

"Well?"

"If—and only if your love survives what I have to tell
you—I will give you my answer."

"It will be the longest month in my life," he admitted.

Her smile was rather uncertain. "In mine too," she
confessed.

"And meantime?"

"Meantime we will both have to wait."

Somewhat to her surprise his response to this was a
sort of grumble of anger. She turned to see that he was
not looking at her but at one of the side boxes.

"What is it?" she asked.

"That man Sefton I met last night. In the box with
Lady Maydock. My God, she is wearing everything but
the Crown jewels. She looks like an advertisement for
something."

The Princess followed his eyes and saw Lady
Maydock in a backless red evening dress and glittering
with diamonds. Beside her, sitting a little behind as
though he were not eager to be seen, was Mark Sefton.
Tonight his face looked hard; the brilliant blue eyes
were veiled.

"What makes you so angry, Brooks?" the Princess
asked him in some surprise.

"Seeing that man with Lady Maydock."

Her brows arched. "What possible difference can it
make to you?"

"Because that is the man Julie loves, according to poor
Bert Wilson. She practically admitted it to him."

"Oh, no!" the Princess exclaimed. "He isn't the right
man for her. It wouldn't be possible. No life for her at
all. It must be stopped, Brooks."

"Will you tell me, my beautiful love, how anyone can
stop a woman falling in love with a man? And Sefton

seems to me to be quite a man, though I don't think much of his taste in women."

"But he won't marry Julie. Never. He told—that is, he is said to be a man who does not care to get involved with any woman. Once bitten twice shy, I believe, is the phrase."

Brooks Mansfield looked at her in some surprise. "How on earth do you know so much about the man?"

"At least," she said, "I feel sure that he cannot harm her in any way. This morning, apparently, he saved her when her horse ran away in Central Park."

"What's that?" He was startled.

The Princess started to explain and broke off as the other boxholders returned to their seats and people filed down the aisles; a few, as usual, arriving to cause a maximum amount of annoyance and disturbance just as the curtains swept open on a swirl of the Prokofiev music. She turned to give all her attention to the stage, and thus avoided returning the gushing wave of a hand and the kiss blown to her by Lady Maydock.

iii

Lisa Maydock settled back in her seat and turned to Mark. "The Princess saw me. I know perfectly well that she saw me. She practically cut me dead."

Mark shrugged.

"I might as well have come with a zombi," she declared, and someone in the next box made an indignant shushing sound.

"I'm still waiting to know why you insisted on my accompanying you here tonight," he said.

Again there was a shushing sound and people turned to frown at the couple who were disturbing the performance by their talking.

Impatiently, Lady Maydock got up and at the gesture Mark put an ermine cape over her shoulders. She was the kind of woman who would ignore discomfort to display ermine even on a mild September night. He followed her out of the box. Still silent, he accompanied her as she began to pace restlessly along the corridor behind the boxes. An occasional usher looked in surprise as they passed. Otherwise no one paid any attention. The muted sounds of the music came through the wall.

"Well?" he asked at last, bored by this pointless delay, eager to get on to something concrete.

She looked at him. "Well?" she asked, with a challenge in her voice.

He ignored the challenge. He shook his head. "No," he said in a tone of finality, "let's skip all the nonsense, shall we? You aren't in love with me, Lisa. For my money, you've never loved anything in your life but those," and he made a disdainful gesture toward the diamonds that glittered at her throat as her cape swung open. "So why? Why this insistence on seeing me tonight? Why that touching little scene at the Maskers Ball when you flung yourself into my arms?"

"Haven't you any heart, Mark?" Her voice trembled with emotion.

He laughed. "About as much as you have," he assured her. "Again I ask—what is this all about? What are you attempting to prove? What do you want with me?"

Her voice trembled again, this time with sheer exasperation. "Oh, you're impossible!"

"About last night," he began again patiently.

"What's the matter? Afraid I might damage your reputation?" She mocked him openly. Then she laughed, a cruel little laugh. "That touching scene, my dear Mark, was staged for the benefit of the wide-eyed and impressionable little Julie Bryce. She lost her head over you on the ship. A blind man could have seen what was happening to her. And she just happened to be out looking at the view with that devoted and idiotic red-haired swain of hers last night when I persuaded you to go out with me. I gave her something to think about."

"Why?" At something in his voice, a savage tone she had never heard before, she took an involuntary step backward.

Then she recovered herself. "Dear me!" she drawled. "Can it possibly be that old stony-heart has a weak spot, after all? Can it possibly be that you are interested in that silly girl?" Her eyes glittered, her face was alight with calculation. "Well, well," she said softly.

"I warn you," Mark said, "to hold your vicious tongue about Julie Bryce."

"My, my, aren't we gallant! Well, my dear Mark, if there are warnings going around, I'll give you one. See that the little Bryce minds her own business, that she doesn't dabble in things that don't concern her. Get her out of town if you have to elope with her—and she'd probably jump at the chance."

Something in his face brought her to a full stop. He took hold of her arm, and even through the thickness of the fur cape she was aware of the pressure. "What are you getting at?" His fingers tightened. "Tell me the truth, Lisa."

"Keep an eye on that girl."

"What do you have against her?"

"Nothing at all. But I have a friend who has ideas, a lot of ideas. Just remember. Get her out of town, get her away from here or God help her!"

"If anything happens to Julie Bryce," Mark said, his eyes blazing, "God help you, Lisa, for nothing else will. I mean that. I'll track you down if I have to go to the South Pole to find you."

"Because you love her?"

He made no reply.

"Who are you, Mark? What are you?"

He looked at her until her eyes shifted away from his. "I'm surprised that you don't know me. I am Nemesis."

iv

It was a relief to Mark when Lisa Maydock jerked her arm away from his hand and went swiftly down the stairs and out of the theater. He followed and hailed a passing cab for her. She got inside and pulled the door shut so fast that his fingers were nearly caught. He looked after her thoughtfully, and then he yawned. God, what he would give for a night's sleep! Then he straightened tired shoulders. It had been a wearing day.

He recalled the panic rush in which he had set off for Central Park to find Julie; the minutes in which he feared for her safety; the walk in which he had come so

close—so close to her. But that was not for him. He had
sent her back to her aunt with a warning to go away.
There seemed to be nothing else he could do.

That afternoon, at the Metropolitan Museum, he had
paused, as he had been instructed to do, to look at Rosa
Bonheur's *Horse Fair*. It was not a favorite picture of his
but his job was to obey orders, though he was given a
good deal of latitude in the way in which he carried
them out. A middle-aged woman was sitting on a canvas
stool making a wildly inept copy of the painting. She
turned in annoyance to look at the intruder behind her.

She spoke, her lips barely moving. "Pennsylvania Station, waiting room, eleven o'clock tonight. Don't dress."

For a few minutes more, until a group of people
appeared at the farthest door, Mark stared at Rosa
Bonheur's big canvas. Even his job, he thought, had its
lighter moments. He was amused by the efforts of the
government agent to copy the painting, a task that
visibly defeated her and led to some caustic comments
from the people who had stopped, as people always do,
to watch anyone paint. When the group left the gallery
he wandered along behind them.

He had hoped to catch a little sleep during the afternoon, before the night's meeting, but Lady Maydock's
peremptory call had demanded that he escort her to the
Royal Ballet.

"You'll be sorry if you don't make it, Mark," she
warned him. "I'm sticking out my neck for you. I won't
do it twice."

After that, he had been unable to sleep or to rest,
trying to guess what it was that would lead her to "stick
out her neck." It wasn't like her. Not like her at all.

Now, at least, he knew the score. Dishonest, unscrupulous, vulgar, probably criminal, all these things Lisa
Maydock undoubtedly was. The brains of an ugly conspiracy. That is, if he was right about her. And yet she
was taking a horrible chance by warning him about Julie
Bryce. That meant there was one crime at which Lady
Maydock balked. She might be too unimaginative to
realize what dope addiction did to people. But there
appeared to be one crime at which Lady Maydock
stopped. Murder. She did not want anything to happen

to Julie Bryce; not, at least, if she herself were to be involved in the crime.

Mark hailed a cab and returned to his house on Gramercy Park, where he removed his dinner clothes and changed rapidly to shabby slacks and a loud sport shirt. He tossed a leather jacket over his shoulder and pulled on glasses with wide amber frames, but the lenses, if anyone had examined them carefully, were as clear as crystal.

At at quarter of eleven he mingled with the crowd in Pennsylvania Station, people milling around, weary theater-goers waiting for suburban trains, travelers preparing to cross the continent to the West Coast; important-looking executives and weary salesmen carrying back-breaking sample cases. There were anxious women making their first train trip and requesting the same information over and over; tired children whimpering to their more tired mothers.

Two men were standing in front of a board that indicated train arrivals and departures. One of them was in overalls. The other carried a suitcase and had the harried look of the nervous traveler.

Mark drifted up to them, glancing at a newspaper he had bought at a newsstand.

The man with the suitcase said, "West Ninetieth Street. Number 760, Apartment B," and looked anxiously at the clock.

"Okay," Mark said, his lips barely moving. He went toward the long passage that led to the West Side subway.

How long, he wondered, as he walked along the passage, listening automatically for the sound of following footsteps, searching the platform, as always the last passenger to board the train, had he done this cloak and dagger sort of thing? Too long. He wondered what it would be like to be at home on his ranch, the day's work behind him, the night air crisp and cold and fresh, without smog, uncluttered by human beings. A night when he could have had dinner—or supper as they would call it out there—with the girl of his choice, and when they could have walked out to look at the stars, which are dimmed in New York by unreal glitter, like that of Lady Maydock's diamonds. A night when he could take the girl in his arms and tell her how much he loved her and she would say that she loved him too.

The train came to a jolt at a station. People stumbled off, weary from a day's work, some people drifted in. The thing about riding a subway at night was that at least you could always count on getting a seat. The train jerked on.

Pull yourself together, Mark told himself. You've been warned. Julie is in danger. What are we going to do to keep her safe?

XII

Apartment B, in a run-down building on West Ninetieth Street, was at the rear of a basement under the stoop of an old brownstone that had once been a comfortable private home. The basement was dirty, the linoleum on the floor seemed never to have been replaced and rarely washed. The ceiling was a forest of pipes, the insulation torn and hanging. There was a smell of cabbage and greasy fish on the stairway. Somewhere from the upper floors came the sounds of a baby wailing, a radio blasting, a girl laughing shrilly, someone trying unsuccessfully to play a steel guitar.

Mark had taken all the usual precautions to reach the meeting place but even now that he was in the basement he waited, counting slowly to forty. Apparently no one had followed him. He walked swiftly to the back of the hall and tapped on the door marked B.

There were half a dozen people in the room, among them a frail-looking girl who seemed to be not more than eighteen years old.

His eyebrows rose in surprise. "Hello, Jane."

"Hello, Mark."

He exchanged greetings with the men and pulled up a chair at the table. This apartment, unlike the rest of the building, was spotlessly clean, furnished more like a committee room than a living room. A long table with chairs lined up on either side took up most of the space.

"We're all here," the man named Harris said. "Let's get going."

"Why this meeting tonight?" Mark asked. "And why here?"

"We have an idea they may be getting onto you," Harris said. "We didn't want you coming to headquar-

111

ters where some interested person might pick up your trail. In fact, you had better stay away from headquarters until this thing is over. Solved one way or another." He added gloomily, "For better or worse."

"Why shouldn't it be solved the way we want?" Mark asked. "Anything new?"

"You might say so." Harris bent over the contraption in front of him on the table and Mark realized that it was a tape recorder. "Charles Norton paid an unscheduled visit to Princess Sobelli this morning at her house. She was able to get her tape recorder working so we have the whole interview."

He played it through while the seven people in the room listened intently. After a moment's pause he re-played it.

"*Curiosity killed the cat*," Norton said, and his footsteps sounded on the floor. In the distance a door closed. The reel wound to a stop.

Harris leaned back in his chair, lighted a cigar, and said, "Well, that's it. The guy might as well have handed us a blueprint. We know when they are moving the stuff and how they plan to dispose of it."

"In a way," Chambers said thoughtfully, "they have played into our hands from the very beginning. It's almost uncanny."

"It was inevitable," Mark pointed out, "if it worked at all. After all, that's the way we wrote the script for them."

"Or, to put it another way, we planted a carrot in front of the donkey's nose and the donkey obligingly followed it."

"And we didn't write the script; you wrote it, Sefton. It has been your plan from the start."

"It has paid off," Mark pointed out. "At least, so far."

The frail-looking girl said, "I've come in late on this one, Mark. I don't know the story."

Harris nodded for Mark to explain. "It's his deal. Let him tell it."

"I don't need to explain to you, Jane," Mark said, "what our major problem always is. We can get the pushers but we can't nail down the people at the top. So the thing goes on and on. I figured that if we could follow one really big transaction through from its inception we would get the top people. What we needed first was to suggest a new way of smuggling in big lots so they would be unlikely to be detected. We looked around for an international business that entails a lot of shipments from various countries, and came up with the field of cosmetics. Of course, to achieve any kind of success, this had to be an operation in which everyone participated. So we talked to Interpol and got their cooperation. After all, the police of every nation—or the majority of them, thank God!—are as interested as we are in putting an end to the dope traffic."

Jane nodded her comprehension.

"The second thing we needed was to find someone of high repute in the cosmetics field who would play along with us. We considered several of them, but it's a choice that had to be right the first time. That was the biggest gamble we had to take. In any case, I finally decided to take a chance on Princess Sobelli. I had a long talk with her, got a promise of secrecy in case she did not care to go through with the program—"

"Can you count on that?" Jane asked.

"Yes, she's a woman of her word. Then I warned her not only of the risk her business credit might run but the risk to her own personal safety. She said it would be worth it. In fact, the biggest surprise to me in the whole operation has been the ready cooperation of Princess Sobelli."

"I've found the answer to that one," Harris put in. "Our people in Italy have dug up everything there is to know about the Sobellis. The Princess's late husband became an addict and died of an overdose of morphine."

"So that's why she was willing to help us!" Mark exclaimed.

"That's why."

"Good. I never quite understood why she was so easy to persuade to take part in a risky business like this. But with her motive, she will probably be glad to take any risk that may be involved. That's a load off my mind."

"I thought you were sure of her."

"Everyone has a breaking point somewhere," Mark pointed out. "Well, the third thing we had to do was to bait the trap. We got rumors started on Wall Street and in business circles that Sobelli Cosmetics, Inc., was in financial trouble and we kept the rumors going. When the news could hardly have failed to get around, we staged that fake burglary and the stealing of the Princess's jewelry and saw that it hit the news media with a great big splash."

"Yes, I saw that," Jane said, "and I had an uncomfortable feeling at the time that it was an insurance swindle. I couldn't understand it because, from what I have heard about her, the Princess has always been a woman of the highest integrity. Never the faintest rumor of scandal about her."

"Of course, we wanted people to think it was an insurance swindle. We had to give the dope ring the impression that the Princess was desperate for money and that she would go to any lengths to acquire it."

"How did you work the burglary?" Jane leaned forward, elbows on the table, chin resting on her clasped hands. She looked as though a strong wind would blow her away, but her eyes, in spite of the carefully drawn blue shadows, were alert and intelligent.

"The biggest problem, of course, was getting the cooperation of the police and the insurance people. Neither of them liked it. But when the insurance people realized that they would not suffer a penny of loss, when the police realized that it was as important for them as it was for us to get hold of the heads of the smuggling ring, they played along.

"That night the Princess took everything out of her safe and left it wide open. She had moved her jewelry into the house a month earlier and waited for a time when her niece would be away from the house so she could not be implicated, in case anything went wrong.

"We met outside the house and she gave me the bag in which she had put the jewelry. That, incidentally, is now lying safely in my deposit box at the bank. When she returned home that night from a dinner party, she 'discovered' the theft, put in the alarm, and the police played along so that her servants would not question the fact of the theft but more suspicious people would doubt that it had really occurred."

From then on they had taken all the precautions they could to close the trap as soon as someone took the bait. Tape recorders were set up at the Princess's town house and at her country house and, of course, in her office.

The first sign of interest came with a telephone call stating that the caller was aware the Princess was bankrupt and that she had been guilty of collecting insurance under false pretenses. If the story got out she would be dishonored and her business would be on the skids. The Princess acted as though she were greatly frightened. What did the caller want in order to guarantee his silence? He explained that he would like to make use of her palace in Florence to store some valuable goods.

She hesitated, pretended to refuse, yielded to pressure and fear. As a sign of good faith she put keys to the palace and a note instructing Giuseppe, the caretaker of the palace, to admit the person presenting the letter in an envelope and mailed it to a box number at General Delivery in the main post office.

The government men had watched the box, had seen Charles Norton remove the keys and letter, and had taken pictures of him when he did so. From that time on he had been followed closely, both in the United States and later when he went to the Near East to collect the dope and on to Florence, where he deposited it at the palace. According to his instructions, the Princess ordered perfume bottles made in Florence. These had an odd design and were opaque with a hidden compartment. They were to be delivered to the palace where they could be filled with heroin and then sent to the United States along with the compacts and lipsticks which she also ordered and which, of course, were quite innocent and just what they purported to be.

Mark had been the operative who picked up Norton's trail in Florence and then, in case the latter noticed him and became suspicious, he turned him over to another agent. On a hunch, Mark himself had followed Lady Maydock, whom he had seen several times in Florence with Norton and who had, since he had first met her a few years earlier, acquired a fortune in diamonds. He had been on the ship with Lady Maydock on her return to the United States. He soon realized that she was keeping an eye on Julie Bryce, Princess Sobelli's niece, who had, most unfortunately, happened to pay a visit to the palace on the very day when Norton had made his deliveries.

"So it became increasingly apparent to me," Mark said, "that Lady Maydock was in this thing. And, judging by the diamonds, the major profit was hers. Certainly Norton shows no evidence of getting anywhere near as big a cut. Like the Maydock woman, he is the kind who would splurge. I figured Norton as a contact and general handyman. But Lady Maydock is the one we're after. Unhappily, while we've got the goods on Norton, as we've followed him step by step from his first contact with the Princess, we haven't an ounce of proof against Maydock. Just suspicion, and you can't convict anyone on that."

"You'll get the proof if anyone can," Harris said, in a tone of confidence.

"Sometimes," Mark admitted gloomily, "I think it would take a miracle."

"You've performed miracles before." Harris refused to be discouraged.

"The queer thing is that she tipped her hand tonight," Mark said. He explained how she had insisted that he accompany her to the ballet. "I couldn't make it out. She was upset. The first time I knew she was capable of having her nerve break. But what she had to say, when she finally got down to it, underlines what you heard Norton say on that tape."

"Unfortunately," Mark said, "when Julie Bryce took it into her head to visit the palace she threw a monkey wrench into the works. Once Norton found out who she was, he was worried. He suspected the Princess of planting the girl there to find out who he was and what he was doing. So he began to rewrite the script. He broke the original agreement and staged a public meeting with the Princess at the Maskers Ball, coming out in the open to warn her that she had a hell of a lot to lose if she didn't go on playing the game his way."

"Do you mean the girl?" Jane asked.

"Lady Maydock," Mark tried to keep his voice emotionless, "said that Julie Bryce had to be got out of the way. One of her friends has ideas about Julie. Lady Maydock said," and he cleared his throat, "she was sticking her neck out to tell me that much. And, of course, she was. She had a terrific decision to make. Naturally she could always deny having made it. There were no witnesses. But even so it was a big risk."

There was unbroken silence in the room for a few moments. Then Mark went on, "I have always regarded her as a really evil woman, but she balks at murder, and apparently her partner Norton doesn't. At least he wouldn't hesitate if he thought Julie was a danger to him. Princess Sobelli has tried to persuade her niece to go away. I have tried."

He remembered Lady Maydock's mocking suggestion that he elope with Julie. At this moment, after hearing Norton's ugly threat on the tape recorder, it seemed to him that he would give all he possessed to carry her away to safety.

He said aloud, "How are we going to keep Julie safe?"

"That," Harris explained, "is why we got Jane Forrest to sit in with us tonight. It is practically impossible for a man to do a satisfactory job at tailing a woman. She goes to buy clothes or get her hair done or any number of things where a man is completely out of place. And Jane, if I do say it, is one of the best in the business. I ought to know. I trained her myself." He smiled affectionately at the fragile-looking girl with the soft blond hair, the dark blue shadows under her eyes, the pale coloring, all of which spoke of poor health.

No one looking at Jane would believe that she was one of the most competent agents the government used in uncovering narcotics rings. With her carefully arranged makeup she could easily pass for an addict. She looked helpless and sickly. Actually, she had superb health, she was an expert at judo, accurate with a gun, and far more able to take care of herself than are most men. So far as Harris knew, the girl had nerves of steel.

"So Jane is going to keep an eye on Julie," Mark said with a sigh of relief. "I'll feel a lot better, knowing that. At least, judging by Norton's talk with the Princess, this won't go on much longer. We seem to be approaching a climax of some sort."

"This waiting is such hell," Chambers complained. "Can't we pull in Norton now and prevent him from doing anything violent to the girl?"

"We could, but if we do we would lose our case, and, bluntly, we are aiming at something more important than the girl, more important than her life because it involves the lives and the health and the reason of many people, not to speak of the criminal activities to which dope addicts are driven in order to get the stuff. No, it is out of the question to haul in Norton now. We want to get these people dead to rights. There must not be a single loophole for a clever defense lawyer. We all know the risk, but we want to get a picture of Norton's men packing that stuff in the palace; we want a picture of them arranging to distribute the stuff from the factory of Sobelli Cosmetics, Inc.," Harris said. "Nothing else will be sufficient to pin this lot down permanently and break up the ring."

"How are you handling the factory end of it?" Mark asked. "That could be a very slippery business."

Harris nodded toward a burly-looking man who might have been a truckdriver and actually was a lawyer who had given up his law practice and turned to fighting the drug traffic because it afforded more action.

"You know each other? Mark Sefton. Julian Thompson."

The two men shook hands. Thompson had a pleasant smile. "I've been following your exploits for some time, Sefton. We could use more men like you. It's nice to know you're on our side of the fence."

"What's your part in this?" Mark asked.

"I'll cover the factory in New Jersey. Tomorrow, as a matter of fact. Some time, later tomorrow or the next day at the latest, the man Norton selects for the job will probably be sent over. I'll have a few hours in which to set up tape recorders and cameras, and arrange the best places to conceal our men. We'll smuggle them in well ahead of time. We're going to get these devils cold." He had a cheerful assurance that eased tension in the room. He too, Mark thought, was a good man to have on our side of the fence.

Chambers sighed so deeply that everyone laughed.

"What's wrong?" Harris asked with a grin. "Still lamenting because we can't pick up Norton right now?"

"I was just realizing what a big operation this is. We've got Interpol as well as our own men ready to photograph everything that goes on in the Sobelli palace in Florence. We've got the New York police and the insurance men working with us. We've got the Sobelli factory bugged and policed, or we soon will have. And we've got Jane Forrest to keep an eye on Miss Bryce."

"Oh, that reminds me," Chambers said, "the Princess sent word, when she passed on the tape recording to agent Feltman, that she believed, in view of Norton's threats, she should have at least one agent in her office. She is planning to give her secretary a week off in which to buy a trousseau or something, and she suggested that an operative who is trained in stenography replace her. We've briefed Florence Gates and she will report for duty in the morning."

Harris looked around him. "Is there anything more to discuss or can we adjourn?"

"I would like to remind you," Mark said, "that the danger threatening Julie Bryce is very real. Lady Maydock would never have risked tipping her hand, if she was not terrified of involvement in murder. For the kind of money she has been hauling in she is probably willing to risk prison, but not prison for life."

Jane leaned forward impulsively, smiling at his distress. "It's all right, Mark. I'll keep an eye on your girl for you."

His smile warmed his hard face, made his eyes glow. He took her hand. "Thanks, Jane."

The slim-looking hand gripped his firmly, reassuringly.

XIII

"The time," a voice from an over-loud radio announced as Mark shut the door of Apartment B behind him, "is now twelve o'clock."

There was no one in the badly lighted basement, no one on the uncarpeted stairs that led to the first floor. Mark peered through the grimy glass in the door. There was no one in sight out of doors. He slipped out quietly and closed the door behind him. The others were to follow at short intervals, so that they would not be seen leaving the place together.

He took his time filling his pipe, while he looked up and down the street. To the west there were car lights on the Henry Hudson Parkway, lights across the dark river on the Jersey side, a few scattered lights in apartments. On this long and dingy block the streetlights seemed dim and far apart.

At the curb in front of the brownstone house some large garbage cans had been rolled. Mark lighted his pipe and then turned his head sharply. Surely there had been movement behind one of the cans. Then something stirred and he relaxed when he saw a cat moving away. Only a cat on the prowl.

He started to walk east, thinking about the meeting, about Jane's promise to look after "his girl." Jane was a whole army in herself. Nevertheless he was uneasy. He had a curious discomfort between his shoulder blades. He had had this feeling before and had learned to respect it. There was someone following him, someone watching him. He wheeled suddenly, too fast for the crouching figure that had begun to straighten up behind the garbage cans to duck out of sight.

Mark reached him in a few long strides, jerked him

120

up with one hand inside his collar, so that he was choking. "Well?" he demanded. "What do you want with me?" He realized that his captive could not get enough breath to speak, and after tapping him lightly to see whether he was armed, he let go of the collar but took hold of his right arm and twisted it behind his back. "Don't thrash around like that, man, or you'll break your arm."

The man whom he had caught was young, with red hair and a homely but pleasant face. Just now his expression was a combination of wry amusement and embarrassment at his predicament.

"Okay, Mr. Sefton." He grinned without rancor. "I'll come quietly."

"Who are you?"

"My name is Bert Wilson."

"And what have you been doing?"

"Trying," Bert admitted, "to keep an eye on you."

"What's your job."

"Newspaper reporter."

"Oh, my God!" Mark exclaimed in horror. "Here, we have got to talk about this. Whatever you think you may have uncovered you are not to print it. There's no story for you."

"Oh, isn't there?"

A cab stopped to unload passengers and Mark hailed it, still holding Bert's arm, though he had relaxed his painful grasp. He shoved Bert into the taxi, got in behind him, and gave the Gramercy Park address.

Neither man spoke on the long ride, but Bert eyed Mark thoughtfully, his expression perplexed.

When they had reached Mark's house he took Bert into the living room and waved him toward a chair. Bert looked at the comfortable furniture, the wood-burning fireplace, the shelves of books, and the record player, then back at his host, a baffled frown between his brows.

Mark pulled up a chair facing him and relighted his pipe. "Well, Mr. Wilson, I think you have some explaining to do."

Bert said bluntly, "I've been following you most of the day, Mr. Sefton. I got your address from the telephone directory, picked you up when you came back here, apparently from riding, and I've been watching you ever since. I saw that phony meeting at the Metropolitan Museum with the woman who can't paint; I got a seat for the ballet and followed you when you left with Lady Maydock. Then I trailed you to that place on Ninetieth Street."

Disturbed as he was at the idea of a reporter getting wind of his activities before the case was solved, Mark grinned appreciatively. "You're pretty good, you know. I had no idea that I had picked up a tail until the last minute. But why did you think you would get a story out of my activities?"

"I'm not looking for a story, Mr. Sefton. Actually, Mr. Brooks Mansfield, a friend of Princess Sobelli and of my editor, arranged for me to get a few days' leave so I could keep an eye on you. Though that, of course, wasn't what he told my editor."

"This is all very flattering," Mark said dryly, "but may I know just why I have aroused so much interest in Mr. Mansfield and you?"

Bert was young enough to flush at the older man's mocking tone, but his eyes were steady and direct. "He loves Princess Sobelli. I love Julie Bryce. I've always loved her. I don't mean," and he made an oddly desolate little gesture, "that gives me any privileges where she is concerned. But I care very much about what happens to her. That's the way Mr. Mansfield feels about the Princess, so we've sort of, well, pooled resources."

Mark was meeting his level glance with equal steadiness now. "And what have I to do with Julie Bryce?"

"I don't know. But I don't want her hurt. Something about the whole Sobelli setup stinks. I don't want Julie involved. But she's so loyal—and then I could see—"

"Well?" Mark prompted him again.

"I don't want her hurt," Bert repeated, though that was not what he had started to say.

"Are you suggesting, by any chance, that I would hurt her?"

"I don't know. It's just as simple as that, Mr. Sefton. I don't know. But Julie—she's impressionable and—I don't have any right to ask, but do you love her?"

"You have no right at all to ask," Mark agreed. "But, for what it's worth, I do love her."

"And what is it worth?" Bert's eyes were still steady and probing.

"Nothing at all, except to me. There is nothing I can do about it. Nothing at all."

ii

Another night had gone and the sun was rising. The morning light picked out the trees in Gramercy Park, first giving them shape and then color. It reflected on the iron fences. It made the lamps burning in Mark Sefton's living room seem pallid. He got up to switch them off, moving a little stiffly.

"Well," he said, stretching himself and smiling at the red-haired young man in the chair across from him, "this has been quite a session."

Bert got up. "I hope I don't need to assure you that none of this will leave the room."

Mark's smile broadened. "I would never have talked like this if I had not trusted you."

"I—" Bert began awkwardly. He went on gruffly, to hide his embarrassment and pleasure at this tribute. "Thank you."

"But," Mark went on, "I can tell you this. If things work out as we both hope they will, you can have the scoop of a lifetime for your paper. The whole story. We want to make the thing public, anyhow, on Princess Sobelli's account. For the sake of her business and her reputation we want to have her completely exonerated of any share in this thing, so no possible doubt can be left in anyone's mind."

"That will be fine," Bert said with so little enthusiasm that Mark looked at him in surprise. Bert grinned. "That promise of a big story doesn't sound as wonderful as it would have eight hours ago. After listening to you all night I've had a change of heart."

Mark looked somewhat alarmed. "What does that mean? Wait. Don't tell me yet. It's—Great Scott, it's nearly seven. We've talked all night. I don't want to wake my man, who keeps tough enough hours, but I'm good at frying potatoes and scrambling eggs. That suit you? And coffee? Gallons of coffee?"

"Sounds swell," Bert said in some surprise, and followed him out to the unexpectedly modern kitchen. He watched his unpredictable host nonchalantly tie a large apron over his shabby slacks and loud sport shirt, measure out coffee and slice potatoes.

"I used to do this out on my ranch," he explained, "when we went on a roundup and the cook on the chuck wagon got sick. And I could make a stew that would have you drooling."

"That's really the life you love, isn't it?" Bert said. During the long heart-to-heart talk that had gone on for so many hours he had heard a lot about the ranch.

"That's the good life, at least for me."

"Why don't you go back to it?" Bert asked. "This is no job for a man who wants to settle down and marry, unless he finds a girl who can live the same hazardous kind of life and like it, and that, I suppose, is impossible."

"I haven't thought of marrying," Mark said, his manner unexpectedly reserved.

"Forgive me but you must have thought of it," Bert said quietly, "after you met Julie."

"I told you that Julie is not for me," Mark said. "I couldn't do that to Julie, expose her to a life without security, tied to a man in a dangerous occupation. Even if I had a chance with her."

"The thing is," Bert said, "that you do have a chance. Every chance. I'm thinking of her happiness when I say you could have her and the good life you long for on your ranch. I saw her face when you were dancing with her. I knew then you were the rival I couldn't beat."

Mark's back was turned while he busied himself turning the potatoes, scrambling the eggs. He said, his voice muffled, trying unsuccessfully to keep it light, "You should taste my flapjacks some time. They're the real *spécialité de la maison* at the ranch." He served heaping plates, poured coffee, and the two men drew up chairs at the small kitchen table.

"I can't walk out on my job," Mark said at last. "There

is a real need for people in my field. I've done well at it. I don't feel I have a right to step out and say it doesn't matter any longer."

"But suppose," Bert said, "that someone were to replace you?"

Mark passed salt and pepper, cream and sugar, devoted himself to his breakfast. "All right," he said at last, "expound."

"I told you I'd had a change of heart, seen a great big dazzling blinding light tonight. You see, I picked the newspaper field because I thought nothing in the world could be as interesting and exciting as digging up the news. Life at firsthand. But tonight I realized it isn't life at firsthand; it simply reports the firsthand living. In your field you see more life, have more adventures—" He broke off as Mark held up a protesting hand.

"Wait a minute! Hold your horses, Red. Adventures belong on television. Leave them there. I can remember talking to a scientist once after he had made an extremely perilous tour, involving among other things going down a kind of waterfall in the dark inside a mountain. I used the word adventure and he nearly blew my head off. A scientist, he told me, doesn't have adventures unless he has done some damned poor planning. Adventures are strictly for amateurs."

"Call it what you will," Bert said. "Oh, don't think I miss the point. But I feel right now that I would like to abandon reporting and go into the bigger job of hunting down the dope peddlers."

"And what about Julie?" Mark asked bluntly.

"I told you she is not for me. She made that very, very clear. I knew how hopeless it was because she was so genuinely sorry for me."

"And if she were for you?"

Bert had no hesitation about that. "If I had a chance, one single chance out of a million, of winning her, I'd take that." He waited while Mark refilled his coffee cup. "How about you?"

There was a long pause. "I don't know," Mark said at last. "I don't know. There has never been time for love in my life."

"Whose choice is it to be, Mr. Sefton? Yours or Julie's?"

"First," Mark told him, "there is a job to do, and that is to keep Julie safe. The operative who has been assigned to her is a wonder but even so I won't rest until the whole thing is over."

"At least," Bert said, "as long as I've been given time off I can act as an extra bodyguard."

"That's an idea. I'll get in touch with Jane Forrest, our operative, and describe you so that she won't have you in handcuffs before you know it for following them around."

"But how will I know her? Of course, I can guess what she must be like. A big strapping masculine wench, who looks more like a policeman than a woman."

There was amusement in Mark's eyes. "You keep an eye on Julie," he suggested, "and let Jane find you for herself." He laughed outright. "I think you are going to get the surprise of your life."

XIV

Julie was dancing with Mark. The ballroom in which
they danced seemed limitless in size, with transparent
walls through which could be seen varied landscapes.
There were Persian gardens filled with roses; there was
moonlight in a broad path on the ocean on which they
could have strolled; there were mountains soaring to the
sky, whitecapped and serene; and always there was
Mark, holding her lightly but securely, guiding her
steps, smiling down at her.

Now he was writing something. "Someday you may
need me," he was saying in his deep voice.

"I will always need you," she told him shamelessly.

There was a faint click and she opened her eyes to see
the maid standing in the doorway. Oh dear, she
thought, I didn't want to wake up. Not just then. I
wanted to go on dreaming.

Aloud she asked, "What time is it?"

"Nine o'clock. You asked to be called," the maid reminded her. "You have an appointment for a shampoo
and set at ten."

When she had bathed in scented water and dressed,
she brushed her hair high on her head and fastened it
with a comb. She smiled impudently at the girl in the
mirror. "You know," she confided to her image, "someday
I'm going to make that dream come true. Look out, Mr.
Mark Sefton, because here I come. Darned if I am not
going to try to get my man. Why should that timorous
May Williams be the only one?"

She was laughing when she left the house and started
walking briskly toward the Sobelli shop on Fifth Avenue. More than one person turned for a second look at
the girl with the big brown eyes, the softly curving

mouth that seemed on the verge of smiling, the lovely erect carriage.

She exchanged friendly greetings with the doorman and went swiftly toward the elevator. To her surprise there was a new secretary at May Williams's desk, a tall, dark, sleek-looking woman in her middle thirties. As Julie came into the office the newcomer summed her up in a long look that took in everything from head to foot. It was, Julie thought, as though her appearance was being carefully memorized, item by item.

May Williams, who was explaining her filing system, turned to smile at Julie. "Miss Bryce, this is—uh—"

"Florence Gates," the newcomer said. "How do you do, Miss Bryce?"

Julie smiled at her but looked at May in surprise and some concern. "You aren't leaving, are you?"

May laughed. "The most wonderful thing has happened! Your aunt is giving me a leave of absence to get," she glanced at Miss Gates, "uh, you know."

"Oh, grand! I have to get my hair done and then we can get started." She noticed the change in May's appearance and said, "You've had a permanent, haven't you?"

May's hair had been shaped, cut shorter than it had been, given a rinse that made it seem brighter, and a soft permanent with only the suggestion of a wave.

May groaned. "I'm getting some more work done this morning, too. That Antoine! The man is a slave driver."

"What has he done?" Julie asked in surprise.

"What hasn't he done?" May turned to the sleek Miss Gates. "Are you sure you understand the details? If you have any questions, you can reach me for the next hour or so down at the shop. After that, I can call you some time during the afternoon."

"Thank you, Miss Williams, but I doubt if that will be necessary. I'm sure there will be no difficulties."

The two girls were silent going down in the elevator and paused at the reception desk to greet the girl in charge and went into the famous salon, with its silver carpets and drapes and its rose leather chairs and fittings, the long mirrors before which women were sitting. Farther along there were dryers with comfortable chairs beside small tables containing ashtrays, coffee, magazines. Beyond, women were having shampoos and facials, manicures and pedicures.

"Mr. Paul is taking you, Miss Bryce," the receptionist said, "and Mr. Antoine is waiting for you, Miss Williams." She looked in surprise at the secretary who was coming for a second day in succession, though she had never put in an appearance before.

"That man!" May muttered.

"What's wrong with him?" Julie asked. "Aunt Georgia regards him as her best operator. She always goes to him for her permanents."

"Operator! I thought perhaps he would cut my hair or create a new hairdo or something like that."

"Well, didn't he?"

May laughed. "That's just the opening wedge. He looked me over and said that I would have to lose five pounds. No candy. No dessert. I have to go to dancing class two nights a week because I don't move gracefully. He is making me exercise to improve my posture. I was so stiff this morning that when I tried to get out of bed I creaked like a rusty hinge."

Julie began to laugh.

"Today, he's going to start experimenting with makeup and begin applying skin food. Beauty culture seems to be a career."

"But, May," Julie said between gusts of laughter, "that is probably what you've been writing from Aunt Georgia's dictation for three years. Didn't any of it stick?"

"Not until it was applied to me," May admitted. She giggled. "What we don't tell people is that the pursuit of beauty is halfway between army discipline and a torture chamber." As Mr. Antoine came in search of her she waved her hand, said gaily, "Dying we salute you." She went down the room and into a small cubicle.

After Julie's hair had been shampooed, she sat before the long mirror, watching the deft fingers of the operator winding the curls. In the next chair there was a pale young girl with long fair hair, who looked as though she had been through some serious illness, her cheeks were so colorless, her eyes so shadowed. Only her mouth was a brilliant red that made her seem even paler. Julie realized that the girl was aware of her scrutiny and her eyes dropped in embarrassment. What would Aunt Georgia think of her, staring at a customer in the shop?

The operator at the next chair was studying his customer carefully. "It's rather long," he suggested. "Not many young ladies are wearing it that length now unless they are still in high school or—uh—"

The girl smiled. "Of course, it wouldn't look so awful, I suppose, if they ever washed it."

"Shall I cut it to shoulder length?" the operator suggested. "Hanging straight like that it doesn't do anything for you."

"Do whatever seems best to you." Again the girl looked away from her reflection to study Julie and their eyes met. The girl smiled faintly. Julie was puzzled by her. There was something odd about the girl's manner, her frail appearance contrasted with the hard intelligence in her eyes.

She was startled by a shrill little cry of synthetic delight. "My dear! How delightful to see you again."

"Good morning, Lady Maydock." Julie tried to impart more cordiality into her voice than she felt, but even so the result was not very convincing.

The older woman wore a suit of English tailoring, no hat on her fair hair, a sable scarf slung over her shoulders. There were diamonds in her ears and, as she removed her gloves, a flash of diamonds on her fingers. She paused beside Julie. "I saw your charming aunt last night. Tell me, how did the Princess enjoy the ballet?"

"I haven't talked to her this morning," Julie admitted.

"She was accompanied by her faithful squire, Mr. Mansfield, of course." Lady Maydock laughed. "And I was with mine. Oh, I believe you have met him. Mark Sefton. Such a fascinating man!"

"You introduced us on shipboard," Julie reminded her. She spoke to the operator. "Am I down for a manicure too?"

"Miss Louise will give you a manicure, Miss Bryce," Mr. Paul assured her.

Julie watched Lady Maydock move off, after blowing a kiss to the girl in the mirror, and then she saw an interchange of glances between two operators, and the

little twist of chagrin at the mouth of the one who had
been assigned to take care of Lady Maydock. Apparently she was not popular in the beauty parlor.

The reason for this became clear not two minutes later
when the operator, who had removed Lady Maydock's
sable scarf, gave a little exclamation of concern. "Oh, I
am terribly sorry. I'm afraid I've caught the lining and
torn it."

Lady Maydock whirled around, snatched the scarf out
of the operator's hands. "That is a zipper pocket. It is
not to be touched! Understand?"

The operator swallowed. "Yes, my lady. I am very
sorry it happened." Her voice was colorless.

Lady Maydock turned back, and raised her voice so
that it would carry clearly to Julie. "My dear, how
distressed the poor Princess would be if she were aware
of the incompetence of her employees."

Julie looked up to catch the angry expression on the
face of her operator and she smiled sympathetically. "It
takes all kinds."

"Not too many like that, Miss Bryce. Fortunately for
us."

The smile faded from Julie's lips. So Mark Sefton had
spent the evening with Lady Maydock. She should have
known! She had seen the woman in his arms. He had
said that the scene had been intended to mislead and
she had believed him because she wanted so terribly to
believe him. Jealousy was a disgusting trait. And to be
jealous of a woman like Lady Maydock was humiliating.

Where's your pride, Julie? she demanded of herself.
You ought to be ashamed. What were you thinking just
an hour ago? That you were going to get your man! And
what man? Lady Maydock's faithful escort.

She forced herself to drive out of her mind the
thought of Mark Sefton. This was to be May Williams's
golden day and she must not spoil it.

Once more Julie noticed the pale girl beside her and
saw that she was watching Lady Maydock in the mirror.
Unexpectedly the girl sneezed and she opened her
handbag to get a handkerchief. By chance Julie saw the
small gun inside the open bag. Then the bag snapped
shut and Julie wondered what she should do. Ought she

to report the girl? Surely it was against the law to carry a concealed weapon.

She was still wondering what she ought to do when her operator settled her in a comfortable chair, asked whether she would like tea or coffee, and pulled the dryer over her head.

Deafened by the blower she was, at least, unable to talk to Lady Maydock, who was sitting nearby getting a manicure and evidently being disagreeable about the work of the manicurist. Her unpleasant criticisms were reflected on the face of the girl who was working on Julie's nails.

While she was still wondering whether to send a message to her aunt or to consult May as to what should be done about the girl with the gun in her handbag, Julie's attention was distracted by seeing May leaning back almost at full length in a rose leather chair while Mr. Antoine worked on her face. The operator, who seemed to be taking the Princess's assignment to heart, obviously did not approve, as his gestures indicated, of May's choice of colors.

Julie lifted her dryer for a moment and heard the indignant man say, "It looks like something out of the dismal swamp," while May stared in chagrin at her drab green and brown dress. Julie exchanged glances with the manicurist, laughed, and pulled down her dryer.

Her eyes roved around the room. Purveyors of the dream, the man in Paris had said. She thought of the movie actresses who, to judge by early pictures, had not had much initially in the way of looks, but had acquired the illusion of beauty. It was good for women to make the best of themselves. It gave them confidence and a sense of their own value as human beings. A girl in tight jeans and a man's shirt, her hair hanging neglected, unwashed, uncut, lacked a sense of her own quality as a person.

Lady Maydock swept out, leaving, apparently, a very inadequate tip, and waving a kiss at Julie, who summoned up a pale smile.

When she had returned to her chair before the long mirror, the customer with the shadowed eyes was gone, and Julie wondered again, deeply troubled, what she should have done about that hidden gun. Then she saw May standing beside her, watching while Mr. Paul combed out her hair and studying Julie's expression eagerly.

May? Julie looked again. In some unexplained way she had come alive. A discreet makeup had been applied, outlining and darkening her brows and lashes, so that her eyes seemed deeper and brighter. Lipstick had been applied to her mouth, the shade a light and unemphatic one, but revealing the shape of her lips.

Standing behind his charge, looking anxiously at Julie for her approval, was Mr. Antoine.

"Well, well!" Julie exclaimed, greatly pleased.

"I hardly know myself," May admitted.

"You ain't seen nothing," Julie assured her. "Here we go to raid the stores."

ii

Sitting in the fitting room, Julie kicked off her shoes with a little groan of relief and watched critically while a clerk lifted the dress over May's hair, holding it away from her face so as not to get lipstick on the fabric.

"You're so nice and tall that it won't have to be shortened," Julie decided.

"*Nice* and tall! Five feet seven."

Julie grinned at her. "Too short for a model but wonderful for wearing clothes. You can show off the lines better than a small girl."

"That's true," the clerk agreed, "and you're lucky to have such a good figure."

Studying herself critically, May said, "Mr. Antoine is right, darn him! I don't stand well; I'll just have to keep it in mind."

"Stand against the wall, heels touching the wall, then hips, then shoulders, and then the back of your head."

"Ouch!"

"Now walk away like that, feeling tall while you walk."

"But I've never wanted to feel tall."

"High time you did," Julie told her without sympathy.

"And the man was right about my weight, too, confound him!" May muttered, studying her reflection in a side view.

"You'll just have to starve," Julie said mercilessly.

"How have we done on that list?" May asked.

Julie checked it, item by item. "One evening dress, two afternoon dresses, three street dresses, one suit with three blouses, gloves, scarves, the sportswear we picked up at Abercrombie's. You aren't bothering about hats? Good. Then there is nothing left to worry about but shoes."

"Not today," May balked. "My feet are so numb by this time I wouldn't know whether a shoe hurt or not. Worn right down to the ankles." With the clerk's help she removed the new dress, slipped on the brown and green one that Mr. Antoine had so disparaged. She looked at it with new eyes. "It does seem drab," she admitted, caught sight of herself, and straightened up automatically. "You've been—I can't begin to tell you how I feel about the way your aunt has given me time and all that free work in the beauty salon, and you—a whole day of tiresome shopping!"

"It hasn't been tiresome; it's been fun," Julie assured her. "Anyhow, I would never trust you out by yourself until you get more confidence about color."

"Someday," May said, "I'll find a way of thanking you." She gathered up her handbag and gloves. "You know, it's odd the way you keep running into people, isn't it?"

"What people?" Julie asked in surprise.

"At least three different times today I have seen the same girl. She was looking at fishing gear in Abercrombie's, and at blouses in Bonwit's, and I thought I saw her out on the floor here just before we came in to try on."

"That is odd."

"The reason I noticed her specially was because she looked as though she had just got up from a serious illness and I thought a day of strenuous shopping would be too much for her."

"Fair hair, shoulder length, dark shadows under her eyes, skin a pasty white, lips thick with brilliant red lipstick?" Julie asked sharply.

"Oh, so you saw her too!"

"Not in the stores," Julie said, "but she was in the beauty salon this morning. I don't"— She remembered the small gun in the handbag. "I don't like that, May. I don't like it at all. If she is on the floor when we go out, I want to make a telephone call."

XV

The girl was not in sight on the floor. At that moment she was in the fitting room next to the one where May had paused to powder her nose before going out. She waited until the two girls had left, went cautiously out onto the floor, careful to stand out of sight behind a rack of dresses while they looked around for her, and did not emerge until they had stepped into an elevator.

As the dress department was only on the third floor, Jane Forrest did not wait for another elevator. She raced down the stairs and reached the main floor before the elevator had discharged its passengers. She was annoyed with herself, as she knew Julie and May had noticed her. Not that it mattered greatly if Julie Bryce were to know she was being followed; perhaps she might even find it reassuring to know she had a guard for her protection. What bothered Jane was her own inadequate technique.

She paused between the inner and outer doors of the big store, watching the two girls who had stopped to talk for a moment. Automatically Jane looked for taxis. If the girls took one she would have to find another in a hurry. But apparently they were parting here. May gave Julie an impulsive hug and then walked away. Julie turned south, headed probably for the Princess's town house. Jane waited for her to get a quarter of a block ahead and then sauntered in the same direction.

A young man with red hair was close behind the Bryce girl and Jane grinned to herself in amusement. This must be the self-appointed bodyguard of whom Mark Sefton had told her. He had been very much in evidence all day, hovering outside stores until Jane wondered that he had not been picked up on suspicion. He was about as inconspicuous as a clown beating a large drum. Certainly he must have been noticed by the people who were tailing the Bryce girl. The surprising thing was that he had managed to keep out of their sight, ducking around in a way that made Jane want to laugh aloud.

Jane wondered whether she had been as easy for the opposition to spot as their agents had been to her. First, there had been Lady Maydock at the beauty salon. She had followed the girls to Abercrombie's, where she had waited until a big man who looked like a professional prizefighter took over until the girls went to Bonwit's to buy blouses. The second agent had then hung around, looking awkward among so many women customers, until a woman came in and nodded to him. He indicated the girls and went out of the store in relief.

Jane's experience told her at a glance all she needed to know about the woman. Of the three, she would be the most dangerous to Julie because she was, Jane thought, an addict. Driven by her terrible need for the drug, she would obey any orders she was given. Mark Sefton had been right about Julie's peril. Jane's hand tightened over her handbag with its small but businesslike gun. "A woman's toy," one of the men in the department had said contemptuously, but it served its purpose.

Julie was turning onto Park Avenue now and Jane felt sure of her destination. She would be safe for the time being. No one could get at her in the Sobelli house. The next problem was to dispose of the woman who had been ordered to follow Julie and report on her activities and the people she met.

Luck wasn't often with her but it was this time. The woman was looking straight ahead, aware of nothing but Julie. A policeman stood in a doorway. Jane paused beside him, slipped her identification out of her handbag and showed it to him, her hand concealed by her body as she seemed to be peering into a window. With her lips barely moving she indicated the woman and explained the problem.

The police officer started slowly down the street and Jane was free of her assignment for the day. She quickened her step, caught up with the red-haired man.

"Dr. Livingstone, I presume."

He looked at her, a puzzled frown on his face. "I'm sorry, I don't believe—"

"I'm Jane Forrest," she told him, and enjoyed the look of stunned surprise on his expressive face.

"Well, I'll be—" he began. He shook his head. "I don't believe it."

"Miss Bryce is all right now," she assured him. "We'll have a man on the job if she goes out tonight; I'm only on during the day. Shopping is rough for a man because it's so hard for him to remain inconspicuous."

"You're sure she is all right? I must say I haven't seen anyone who took any special interest in her." As Jane grinned at him he challenged her, "Was there anyone?"

"Three." She laughed outright at his look of chagrin. But when he began to hurry, his face worried, she said soothingly, "It's all right, Mr. Wilson. That policeman ahead of us is going to pick up the woman in the black coat—yes, she is one of them. And the worst, if I'm right. I think she's an addict and they are usually unpredictable."

He was disgusted. "You mean to say there were three people following Julie and I didn't spot any of them?"

She chuckled. "Actually, there were five, including you and me."

"There seems to be a lot about this business I have to learn. Look, can't we go somewhere and talk, as long as you feel sure Julie is all right? I'm going at this thing sort of blindly."

"I have an apartment down on Ninth Street," she told him, "if you'd care to come there. I'm off for the day."

"Ninth Street. Then we're neighbors. East or West Side?"

"East. Near New York University."

"Then why haven't I seen you around before?" Bert demanded. He hailed a cab, asked for the number. "Just two blocks from me. I'll be darned. And you've been around all this time?"

He looked incredulously at the fragile girl with the blond hair softly curling at her shoulders, at the big blue eyes so deeply shadowed. "I can't get over it. To think that you—" At her expression of alarm, her frantic gesture of warning toward the driver, he broke off what he had been about to say. He did not speak again until they reached the apartment building.

Jane Forrest had a two-room apartment with one of those minuscule balconies that hold two chairs close together and are overlooked by a couple of hundred people if they are curious enough to look out. But the apartment, with its cream woodwork, its bright rag rugs, its well-filled bookcases and reproductions of good paintings on the walls, was pleasant and light and homelike.

Jane excused herself while he looked around the room. There were venetian blinds to shut out curious eyes at night. Then there was the aroma of coffee and she came back with a tray holding coffee cups and a plate of doughnuts.

"Baked these yesterday," she explained. "That was my day off."

Again he looked at her in surprise. She had taken time to wash her face and she had removed the artificial shadows from her eyes, the thick white makeup, and now she was a healthy-looking girl with a clear glowing skin, bright eyes, and a firm mouth that was pleasantly pink but not with the thick brilliant paste of the earlier part of the day.

She put the cups and plates on the coffee table and went out for the coffeepot. "Cream?" she inquired. "Sugar?"

"Anyone would think," Bert remarked, still rocked off his feet, "that you were any normal girl with a domestic yen."

For a moment there was a hurt expression on her face. "I am just a normal girl with a domestic yen," she told him flatly.

"I didn't mean—"

For some reason which he could not understand she was angry. "I know what you mean. Mark told me over the telephone what kind of person you expected me to be. He thought it was a joke. A girl can be normal and like to keep the place where she lives in nice order and cook a good meal. But sometimes she wants more than that. She needs some kind of life outside her house; and I personally would die in a routine office job or behind a counter in a store or at a factory machine. I want something—something vital to do, something that isn't the same old thing, hour after hour, day after day. Something—unexpected."

"And the danger?"

She hesitated for a moment. "All right," she admitted, "I suppose I like that too. At least I wouldn't quit because of it."

Bert helped himself to another doughnut, drank coffee in silence.

"I suppose you are horribly shocked," she said at last.

"I didn't know there were girls like you. Ever since I talked with Mark Sefton last night I've known that I wanted to go into your field, if they'll have me. What I never guessed was that there might be girls—at least, a girl—who would accept a life like that; gosh, *choose* it, and still look the way you do. Little and helpless and—and sweet."

The girl who had seemed unaccountably angered by his surprise over her appearance, had got over it now. She was smiling. She reached for his cup. "More coffee, Bert?"

"Thanks, Jane. Oh, and before I forget it, what are your days off?"

ii

Late that night Jane Forrest wrote a report on the day's activities. She described picking up the "subject" at the Sobelli beauty salon where Lady Maydock had appeared, had loitered outside when her appointment was over, and had trailed Miss Bryce and Princess Sobelli's secretary, May Williams, to Abercrombie's where she had been replaced by another agent whom Jane described.

The latter had taken up the trail and had followed the girls to Bonwit's, where he in turn had been replaced by a woman whom Jane did not know but who looked like a drug addict. Jane had pointed her out to Officer 876. A telephone call had just reported that he had picked her up. She was Helen Fanes, an old offender, out on probation, and carrying a switchblade in her purse as well as a small quantity of heroin.

Miss Bryce had spent the day accompanying Princess Sobelli's secretary on a shopping trip and had returned home when the shopping was finished. Apparently Norton's threat had been no empty one. If the drug ring was prepared to have three people follow the subject to find out what she was doing and whom she was meeting, they believed her to be a source of potential danger. All security measures in regard to Julie Bryce should be tightened without delay.

Jane finished her report, reread it and corrected some typing errors, and went out to the mail drop in the corridor to send it on its way.

It was an accurate report. It contained, however, no mention of the red-haired Bert Wilson who had, with the help of the prominent Mr. Brooks Mansfield, been trailing Julie for her own protection and who was now aware of Mark Sefton's real identity and the problem involved. The department would not be pleased if it were to learn that Mark had talked so freely to this young man, particularly in view of the fact that he was a newspaper reporter. Enough to make their blood run cold, that was, even though Bert would not betray anything that he had stumbled on.

It was curious how sure Jane Forrest was of that. In her job she did not often encounter men like Bert Wilson, patently honest, somewhat naïve, innately kind. And he had a nice sense of humor too. He had kept her laughing.

While she got ready for bed, Jane thought about Bert. She grinned in amusement over his unconcealed astonishment when he learned her identity, and then the grin faded. She stood looking at herself in the mirror. He had expected to find a big masculine tough sort of woman, a kind of female coal heaver. Well, at least, she didn't look like that. But had she grown hard and unfeminine and coarsened while doing her job? The girl who looked back at her anxiously seemed perfectly normal and completely feminine.

Nonetheless Jane's hour of happiness was dimmed. The men in her department regarded her not as a woman but as an excellent and reliable agent. Bert Wilson, after his first surprise, had regarded her as a girl, and a very attractive one. But don't forget, Jane told herself grimly, he wasn't getting leave of absence today in order to meet you. He wanted to protect Julie Bryce. And I can't blame him, after all. She's so lovely. He's in love with her. And Mark Sefton is in love with her too, whether he knows it or not.

Jane put out the light, but even so her bedroom was light because of the streetlights and the glow of New York. Tomorrow she and Bert would be working together, even if their object was to safeguard Julie Bryce. She and Bert were neighbors. Think of it. They had lived here, within two blocks of each other, for two years and never met. Jane's eyes were wide open in startled wonder. Why, they might never have met at all!

XVI

Mansfield's butler opened the door and the former diplomat came forward eagerly to shake hands with Bert.

"I'm sorry to be so late, sir," Bert told him.

"It's not ten-thirty. I knew you must be busy keeping an eye on Julie."

"Ah—yes, well, I was, sir." It occurred to Bert that he and Jane Forrest had left Julie some six hours earlier and that since then he had been with the agent. One thing had led to another, talking about the government department and the best way to get into it, and about how odd it was that they should turn out to be neighbors. Then, somehow, she had suggested that he stay to dinner. Afterwards they had talked some more, and he had helped with the dishes.

"What's the story?" Mansfield leaned back in his chair, wondering at the younger man's embarrassment. As the silence was prolonged, he looked downright surprised.

"Sorry," Bert said at last, "I was wondering how much I could tell you."

"What on earth does that mean?"

"It is terribly confidential, sir. I was trusted not to give any information to anyone."

"If you have given your word not to tell me something, of course you must keep it." After a moment's pause Mansfield asked, the hurt clear in his voice, "Was it Princess Sobelli who asked you not to explain the situation to me?"

"No, it wasn't. I haven't seen her at all," Bert answered promptly.

Mansfield's face cleared. "Then tell me what you are at liberty to. Or, if you prefer, tell me nothing. You are under no obligations to me, after all. What I have in mind is simply to be of service to Georgia and Julie if I can."

"Well, I can tell you this much. It is true that Princess Sobelli is involved in rather a sticky situation, but it is of her own choice and there is nothing in the least discreditable about it. Rather splendid of her, in fact."

"You don't need to tell me that."

"No, sir. Well, the thing is that Julie is actually in a good deal of danger at the moment. It's a temporary situation, thank God, and while it lasts, every possible effort is being made to protect her. Of course, if she would only go away, it would be the best thing, but she won't. Anyhow, there are two highly trained people keeping an eye on her, one for daytime and one for evenings and nights; he stays in the house, let in by Princess Sobelli after the rest are in bed, and he lets himself out in the morning. And, of course, I'll be working with the daytime agent, in case it should be necessary to divide forces."

He went on to explain that three different people had trailed Julie during her shopping trip with May Williams. As both Mark and Jane had warned him grimly about making any reference to narcotics, Bert said nothing about the last tail being an addict.

There was a long pause while Mansfield thought about the situation. "Do you know what this is all about?" he asked at length.

"Yes, sir."

Mansfield got up to look out at the magnificent view of New York City, from the dark park to the brilliant lights of the great avenues on either side. He came back to resume his chair. "What can I do to help?" he asked simply.

"Not a thing, sir. It's mostly a question of waiting now and, of course, protecting Julie." Bert yawned widely, and Mansfield laughed.

"If you are going to protect her tomorrow you had better get some sleep tonight."

Bert took the extended hand. "Good night," he said.

Out on Central Park South he turned east and started to walk home. He needed exercise and the evening was cool. He wished that he had been able to relieve Brooks

Mansfield's anxiety but he had to keep faith with Mark
Sefton and Jane Forrest. It occurred to him that he had
not mentioned Jane by name. Undoubtedly Mansfield
had assumed that Julie's daytime protector was a man.

Bert was walking more slowly now, avoiding other
pedestrians more by luck than observation, deep in his
thought. Who would ever have believed that a young,
pretty, domestic girl like Jane Forrest would choose a
life of danger and excitement? He hadn't even known
there were girls like Jane. And to think they had been
practically next-door neighbors all this time and he had
not even seen her on the street. At least they would be
working together tomorrow instead of separately. Almost
anything was better if it was shared by two people.

Julie was still, as she had always been, his dream girl.
Lovely and charming and—out of reach. Or perhaps her
unattainability had been a part of her charm. A girl to
be sheltered. But there were girls like Jane Forrest,
looking as though they were helpless, who risked their
lives to protect other people.

Bert began to whistle softly as he walked.

ii

Florence Gates, in her one-room apartment on West
Fifty-fourth Street, looked at her watch in some surprise
and answered the telephone.

"Miss Gates?" said an unknown woman's voice.

"This is Florence Gates speaking."

"You are the Miss Gates who started work today as
Princess Sobelli's secretary?"

"That's right. May I ask who is speaking?"

"I think we'll let that go for the time being," the
woman said with a soft laugh. Florence, raising her
brows, reached for pencil and paper, prepared to record
the conversation. It might be worthwhile.

"Are you interested in making a little money on the
side?"

"Well, I—" Florence hesitated, "I've just started on a
new job and there's a lot to learn. I'm not sure that I'll

have energy enough to take on anything extra in my spare time."

"This would not require more than ten minutes a day and it might pay you—say, a hundred a week."

"Is this a joke?"

"Far from it. If you want to earn some extra money—"

Florence's mouth curved in an amused smile. She said, "Well, of course, I'd love making more money. I am getting married in a couple of months and we have to furnish an apartment from scratch. But I don't know what I could do in ten minutes that would be worth that kind of money to you."

"Have you known the Princess long?"

"Never saw her until today," Florence replied promptly, "when the agency sent me. I'd heard of her, of course, but who hasn't?"

"Do you like her?"

"Not too much," Florence replied, guessing this would be an acceptable answer. "High and mighty. But a job's a job."

The unknown woman could not conceal a note of triumph in her voice. "I think you and I can talk business that would be mutually profitable."

"Just what do you want of me?"

"A report, hour by hour, of what the Princess does, whom she sees, whom she talks to."

"Well," Florence seemed to hesitate, "I suppose I could keep a record of what goes on in the office: her appointments, her telephone calls, her correspondence."

"That's all I'd need."

"But how would I get it to you?"

"Leave your report at six o'clock every evening, starting tomorrow, in a note addressed to George Fairbanks, at the desk of the New Yorker Hotel. Next morning there will be a twenty-dollar bill in your mailbox. A hundred a week for five reports. All clear?"

Florence took her time replying, as though debating with herself. "Well, I—I wouldn't get into any trouble, would I?"

"How could you? You needn't sign anything."

"Why do you want me to do this?"

The explanation at the other end of the wire was

somewhat involved and indicated a struggle between two rival cosmetic firms. If the other firm got the business away from the Princess, Florence would be set up for life in a good job. And she had, the unknown woman pointed out, absolutely nothing to lose, no risk to run. She would be paid, day by day, for her reports.

Florence carefully typed the record of the telephone call and added a paragraph, pointing out that someone at the Sobelli firm was in a position to report on the fact that Princess Sobelli had acquired a new secretary and to provide her name and address. She would try to spot who it was. Then she went to the corner mailbox to drop the report in the slot. Someone from the department would be waiting to see who picked up Mr. George Fairbanks's mail at the New Yorker tomorrow evening. Florence grinned to herself.

She rinsed out stockings and got out clothes for the next day. It would be wonderful to lead a steady, safe, normal life once more, to keep regular hours, to be able to take time to create the kind of home her fiancé had in mind. He was a wonderful guy, she thought, but conventional, and not inclined to approve of anything that was outside the normal nine-to-five routine. He hated her job.

That day in Princess Sobelli's office had been fun. She was aware that she had a good head for business. She had enjoyed herself, enjoyed the routine, the work, the problems involved. To head an outfit like that—she put the idea aside with a laugh. That wasn't for her. Tomorrow she must remember to ask Princess Sobelli to give her the information needed by the unknown woman. The Princess would probably be amused. What a beautiful woman she was! And she would be even more beautiful if that cold façade ever warmed into tenderness.

I'm getting sentimental, Florence decided, turned on her side, and slept.

iii

Lady Maydock set down the telephone in her sitting room at the hotel, lighted a cigarette, and began to walk up and down the floor, her long black velvet culottes flashing as she moved, gold slippers with high heels, the gold blouse cut down to a deep V in front.

Everyone had his price. Georgia Sobelli's new secretary had seemed glad of a chance to earn more money. Needed it to furnish an apartment. Lisa Maydock smiled scornfully. Apparently the woman was fool enough to marry a man who couldn't even afford to furnish an apartment for his bride. Well, the girl's loss was Lisa's gain. She would call Charles and tell him to watch tomorrow at six for the first report at the New Yorker where he was registered as George Fairbanks.

She went over the plan in her mind. Within a few days the operation that had been months in planning would be completed. Tomorrow the perfume bottles would reach the palace. From there they would be shipped by air freight to New York and then sent by truck to the Sobelli factory in New Jersey for repackaging and distribution. It was the biggest deal she had ever conceived. Perhaps she would be wise not to push her luck too far. Perhaps she had better retire when the money came in from the dope. A minimum of three million dollars. Perhaps it would run to five million. She drew a long breath.

There were diamonds at Harry Winston's on which she had set her heart, necklaces and bracelets and one immense and perfect stone that almost rivaled the Kohinoor. Enough to keep her in luxury for the rest of her life.

She might decide to leave New York, spend a few weeks now and then at her husband's English estate because, after all, her marriage had given her a certain social standing she could have acquired in no other way. But she would buy a place on the Riviera and perhaps another in Switzerland.

You could buy anything with diamonds. Absolutely anything. She removed the diamond earrings and held them in her hand, turning them to see the lights catch and glitter, reflecting red and blue and yellow, as they moved. But what could you buy with them that was lovelier than the diamonds themselves? To part with them, even for luxuries, was like pain.

For them she had taken risks that seemed incredible to her now in this comfortable hotel suite, but they had been worth it. Nonetheless she had a nagging feeling that her luck had run out, that it was time to quit. Not that she was afraid that she would make mistakes, but she did not trust her colleague, Charles Norton. She could not understand now why she had found him plausible, why she had been weak enough to draw him into this scheme.

Her hand clenched in exasperation. Why had that tiresome Julie Bryce gone to the palace while Charles was there? Why? Why? Try as she could, Lady Maydock had not been able to get any information from the girl on the ship. It was impossible to tell whether she was honestly ignorant or whether she was concealing information. She had mentioned the palace but ony as a sadly run-down and deserted old place, a part of her aunt's past. Surely she was innocent of any attempt to check on Norton and his activities. But if he believed that she had any suspicions about him—

It seemed to Lady Maydock that there were sharp claws digging into her spine. Murder. Charles would involve her if he were caught himself. And that meant prison. Prison for life. Barred doors. The diamonds out of reach. Forever out of reach. Charles simply had to be convinced that Julie was not involved in the situation. And even if she were, there must be safer ways of assuring her silence.

She lifted the telephone and asked the operator to get her Mr. George Fairbanks at the New Yorker Hotel.

iv

"Charles, this is Lisa."

"Well?"

"On the whole, things are going very well." She reported on her conversation with Princess Sobelli's new secretary. "That should give us a line on what she is doing in case the woman should lose her nerve at the last moment or anything like that. You should get the first report tomorrow evening at six. If it is satisfactory, leave a twenty-dollar bill in an envelope in her mailbox. This is the address."

"All right. How about Bryce? What is she up to?"

"I picked her up this morning and followed her from the beauty salon until Austin was able to take over. Absolutely nothing happened, Charles. It was an ordinary shopping trip. She was helping a girl to select a trousseau and she didn't so much as speak to anyone else."

"Does Austin think it was just a simple shopping trip, too?"

"He followed the girls from Abercrombie's to Bonwit's but he ran into trouble there because they spent a lot of time looking at blouses. It was no place for a man to hang around, particularly a man like Austin who looks like a prizefighter. People notice him. He was terribly conspicuous."

"Well, what happened?" Norton was impatient. "Did Austin just give it up as a bad job and go home? Leave the girls on their own?"

"No, of course not. He got hold of Helen Fanes and told her what to do. She was to follow the girls for the rest of the afternoon."

"Fanes! What the hell did Austin mean by calling her in on this job?"

"I told him to."

"Now she is able to identify one of our people. You know how dangerous that is."

Lady Maydock found herself on the defensive. "I couldn't very well put in a second appearance in one day, and we don't have any women available unless we use one of Them." She didn't need to explain what she meant by "Them." "They have to do what they are told or the supply is cut off."

"This time you've muffed it, Lisa," Norton said in an ugly tone.

"What do you mean?"

"Frank called me a couple of hours ago."

"Frank? The lawyer?"

"The lawyer. Helen Fanes was picked up late this afternoon. She called Frank from the police station, wanting bail."

Lady Maydock felt suddenly cold. She moistened her lips. "What was the charge?"

"Carrying a concealed weapon and having heroin in her possession."

"But—"

"How did they know?" Norton asked.

"Charles, you won't do anything foolish?" There was a hint of desperation in her voice. "Julie Bryce is not involved in this in any way."

"No? The woman we had tailing her was picked up. How do you explain that?"

"It wasn't Julie Bryce! I swear it couldn't be."

"Of course not," he assured her, his mouth twisted in a grin. "I won't hurt the little girl." He laughed and put down the telephone.

XVII

Julie put on a russet tweed suit she had had made in London, a soft white silk blouse, and fastened a plain gold pin to a lapel. She was annoyed by the disconsolate droop of her lips. She must not let herself think about Mark because there was only pain in doing so.

Last night her aunt had startled her by saying, "Julie, I hope you are not being foolish."

"Foolish?"

"Building something romantic out of the fact that Mark Sefton stopped your runaway horse. You are too sensible for that."

"You think it would not be sensible for me to feel grateful to him?"

The Princess had smiled. "I am not talking about gratitude, as I think you know. My dear, Mark Sefton is the wrong man for you. Even if he considered marriage, and I am sure he does not, you would have no happiness with him."

The two had faced each other. "Why are you so sure of that, Aunt Georgia?"

"My dear, there is no place for a wife in the life of such a man. No possibility of happiness with him because there would be no—no real safety."

"Where is there safety?" Julie challenged her. "We could be run over when we leave the house, or fall on a piece of soap in the bathroom and break a hip, or be struck by lightning. Life isn't safe no matter how many safeguards there may be." For a long moment she looked at her aunt. "Anyhow, I think," she said slowly, "I would rather be unhappy with Mark Sefton than happy with anyone else. I don't know what he does and I don't care. I don't know what your dealings with him are and I

152

don't care. I don't know what Lady Maydock's association with him means and I don't care. I love him, Aunt Georgia. I really love him."

And then she had been in her aunt's arms, sobbing wildly. After that, neither Julie nor her aunt had made a further comment about Mark.

Nonetheless, she found herself waiting. He had not said that he would call her; actually, he said he had intended to stay away from her. But every time the telephone rang her heart leaped with hope and dropped again when the caller proved to be someone else.

Looking at her unhappy face, Julie made a rueful grimace. You'll have to do better than that, she warned herself. You look like the chief mourner at a funeral.

So she was smiling brightly when she entered the Colony and went to the table reserved by an old friend. Apparently she had been successful in disciplining her face and her thoughts because her friend exclaimed, "How wonderful you look, Julie! That European trip must have done you a world of good."

"Oho," a girl whispered softly, across the room where she had been watching Julie's table, "do you see what I see?"

Bert who, after a dismayed look at the prices on the menu, was digging furtively in his pocket to make sure he could pay for the lunch, glanced up in surprise. "What's that?"

"Don't look now," Jane warned him, "but the man who came in right behind Julie Bryce is Charles Norton. I saw pictures of him this morning at headquarters. No, don't turn around. He knows you by sight. Fortunately, he doesn't know me."

"But he can't do anything to Julie in a public restaurant," Bert said.

"No, but he can follow her when she leaves. You order for me, will you?" She was aware that he was ill-at-ease about the prices. "I'm not at all hungry," she assured him. "Just an omelet and coffee."

"Where are you going?"

"I'll telephone the office and arrange to have a car brought here. If Norton follows Julie on foot you can

take over, but do be careful not to let him see you. If he
has a car or takes a taxi we can use the car."

Julie, chatting gaily with her friend, caught sight of
the pale girl from the beauty shop, the one who, according to May, had followed them the day before, the
one who carried a small gun in her handbag. For a
moment she lost track of what her friend had been
saying. It simply could not be coincidence that the girl
appeared so insistently on her trail. But what was the
reason for it? She tried to see whether the girl was alone
but there was a heavy woman in between who blocked
her view.

"You haven't heard a word I was saying," her friend
complained, and Julie looked up at her with a start. For
a moment she was sorely tempted to confide that a girl
who was armed with a gun had followed her for two
days. What stopped her was the fear that the pale girl
was in some way associated with her aunt's mysterious
activities, and that by saying anything about her she
might do some injury to the Princess.

As they were about to leave the Colony, a pleasant
voice said, "My dear Miss Brycel This is certainly my
lucky day."

She turned in surprise. "Mr. Norton, isn't it? Let me
introduce you to my friend."

He drifted along with them to the entrance, hovered
politely in the background while Julie and her friend
parted, and then said, "May I have the pleasure of
taking you somewhere? I have my car here."

Julie deliberated only for a moment. Charles Norton
had, she felt sure, some hold on her aunt. Perhaps there
was some way in which she could find out what it was,
some way in which she could help her aunt.

"That would be very kind."

"Where would you like to go? A little ride out of the
city for an hour or so? It's a fine day."

"What fun," she said, and let him help her into the
car.

They were both too absorbed, Julie in planning the
best way to extract information, and Norton in getting
into the line of traffic, to notice a car which, surprising-
ly, had been allowed to double park, and which now

further disregarded the law by making a U-turn and
falling in behind them. If Julie had turned her head she
would have recognized the pale girl at the wheel of the
following car. She would not have seen Bert, however,
because he was crouching on the floor.

Jane Forrest said, "You can get up now. They aren't
looking. In the glove compartment you'll find a cap
which I asked them to send along to cover that red hair
of yours."

Bert sat up, grinning, and pulled the cap over his red
hair. "I should have thought of that myself. Where do you
suppose Norton is taking her?"

"We'll soon find out. In any case, he didn't force her to
go along. She seemed to like the idea."

"Well, I don't," Bert declared. "She dislikes and dis-
trusts the man. It would be like the crazy kid to try to
outsmart him. She's convinced he has some sort of hold
on the Princess and she's so darned loyal she'd try anything to help her."

"She's in for a surprise then," Jane commented dryly.
"They showed me his record this morning. A few years
ago he was involved in a big jewel-smuggling operation.
He got away with it by the skin of his teeth though the
other people involved went to prison. He is not a nice
man for a girl to know, not Mr. Charles Fairbanks
Norton, and he'd be more than a match for a girl like
Miss Bryce."

ii

Julie smiled radiantly at Norton. "How did you guess
that I'd love a ride into the country?"

"After one look at you, I had just a single ambition,
and that was to know you better. If I've started out by
guessing right about what you like, that chalks one up
for me. I suppose people keep telling you how beautiful
you are."

Julie fought back a surge of disgust. She loathed this
kind of blatant compliment, whose obvious insincerity
was a sign of contempt for the recipient. The man was
so conceited he probably thought she would be swept

off her feet by his admiration. Then she reminded herself that she must not betray her annoyance. Her job was to learn more about him.

"You can tell me something I've always wanted to know," she said.

"What's that?"

"Well, I gathered from what you said at the Maskers Ball that you knew Aunt Georgia's husband very well. Do tell me what he was like. When he died I was in boarding school and all I know of him is that wonderful portrait. Was he really as good-looking as that?"

"Very handsome fellow," Norton said.

"A great chess player, I understand."

"The best I ever played with. Way out of my class, of course. So you never knew him. Never visited the palace while he lived there?"

Julie shook her head in regret. "The last few years of his life, by the time I was old enough to get any benefit out of traveling, he was too ill to have visitors. I didn't know what was wrong. As a matter of fact, I never have known."

Norton gave her a sharp glance but she was not looking at him.

"So you decided to visit the place on your own," he said, and Julie folded her hands over her handbag to conceal their trembling. "What on earth made you visit that old wreck? Nothing to see there any more but a few stray pieces of furniture and disintegrating tapestries."

How do you know? Julie wanted to ask. According to you, you haven't been in the palace, you haven't even been in Florence, for years.

"Well, I'd heard such a lot about it and it sounded—a palace you know," she laughed at herself, "after all, it sounds so romantic, and besides it had been Aunt Georgia's home for so long."

"So naturally she wanted you to go there," Norton said.

Julie looked rather ashamed. "The truth is that I didn't tell her I was going. I was just curious, after all, and I was afraid maybe—"

"Afraid she would think you were snooping?" Again she heard that soft tone in his voice. Like—like something lurking, waiting to spring, Julie thought. For some reason her unheralded visit to the palace was important to this man.

"Of course she wouldn't think I was snooping!" She sounded so righteously indignant that Norton was inclined to believe her. "The only reason I didn't tell her at the time was because I didn't want to arouse unhappy memories. She had struggled so bravely to rebuild her life after her husband died. I didn't want to make her think of all that again."

"But you did mention it, you know, at the Maskers Ball, when you thought you had seen me at the palace."

"But that was because you had already referred to her husband, so the harm was done. And anyhow, I was so sure I had seen you there. Such an extraordinary resemblance! And," she looked at the smoke swirling up from his cigarette, "the—the other one was smoking Turkish tobacco too. And someone in the palace had been smoking the same kind. I could smell the smoke. Why I could even see it hanging in the dead air!"

Norton laughed. "Quite an observant little lady, aren't you? Did you go through the whole palace?"

"Just about."

"Even peek in the closets?"

"No, I couldn't because they were locked." In her anger Julie forgot to be cautious. "What on earth were you afraid I would find, Mr. Norton?"

Norton made no reply but suddenly Julie lost her confidence that she could cope with this man, that she could get information out of him. She began to feel frightened. How absurd, she thought. She could take care of herself. She always had.

"Where are we going?" she asked, trying not to show that she was uneasy.

They had crossed the span of the George Washington Bridge, the Hudson River blue and sparkling beneath them, the little red lighthouse brave and gay under the sun. Now they were speeding along Route 4 headed west. Don't be ridiculous, she told herself, aware again of her growing uneasiness. Nothing can happen to you with all these people around.

"Just for a ride," he said easily. "Of course the best

time to see New Jersey is in the spring when all the flowering bushes are putting on a display. But we'll get off the beaten track soon and find a nice country road."

"I think," Julie said in a small voice, "we'd better go back."

Norton made no attempt to check the speed of his car. In fact, he turned on his directional light and moved into the passing lane, picked up from forty-five to sixty miles an hour. She had an uneasy feeling that he was laughing at her, sure he had the upper hand. "So your aunt sent you abroad to check up on her new designs. That's quite a responsibility for an inexperienced young lady. What did you think of them?"

"Oh, my job wasn't as important as that. I'm not really equipped to judge. Anyhow, all I asked about was whether the work was progressing all right, and reported to Aunt Georgia that all was going well."

"And you thought it was?" Again that curious, ugly feeling of something that lurked in the shadows, waiting to pounce.

She made herself laugh. "I could report only on what people told me. But of all the things I heard only one really impressed me."

The car shot ahead as though his foot had pressed hard on the accelerator, and then he slowed to a legal speed. "And what was that?"

"What the man in charge of the Paris branch told me: that they were purveyors of the dream."

"Purveyors of the dream." Norton was amused. "You know, Miss Bryce, that really hits it on the head. Miss Bryce? No, that's too formal. It's going to be Julie from now on. And I am Charles. We are going to be friends, I feel convinced of that. Very dear friends."

Julie made no reply. Instinctively she drew herself as far away as she could on the seat.

"Very dear friends," Norton repeated, not appearing to notice her gesture of withdrawal. For a few moments he was absorbed in thought. "You are Princess Sobelli's only living relation, aren't you?"

"Yes, we just have each other, but for me that is enough."

Only living relation, Norton thought. Obviously the

Sobelli cosmetics business was in trouble at the moment but it could be put back on its feet. The Princess was not likely to marry again; everyone said that. This girl would probably inherit the lot. He glanced at her profile. Really lovely, he thought. There would be no unpleasantness about marrying the girl. A real pleasure, in fact. And since she seemed to be getting herself involved in this thing it would be wiser, perhaps, to marry her than—he did not carry the thought through. No use putting unpleasant things into words if it could be avoided. Much wiser, much simpler to marry her. Wives can't testify against their husbands. And the Princess would not be able to raise any objection. She would not dare. He began to laugh.

"What's so funny?" Julie asked. "Please, Mr. Norton, turn back."

He ignored her plea. "What's so funny? I was thinking of that description: Purveyors of the dream. That's truer than you know. Right on the mark. There are things to be had on the market these days that insure dreams, all right. Deep dreams. Hallucinations that are bigger and brighter than life. Dreams for which people are ready to die—or to kill."

Something in his voice made Julie shiver. It was not dreams like these that the man in Paris had meant. There was something terrifying here.

Norton turned into the slow lane and then onto the exit that led out from the main highway to a side road.

"Where are we going?" Julie demanded, conscious that her voice was shrill with fear.

"There's a little country lane near here," he said, his voice lazy and amused. "A nice place for a quiet, uninterrupted talk."

"Mr. Norton!" She was really angry. "Please take me home!" She had abandoned any idea that she was a match for this man. All she wanted was to get away from him. She understood now, she thought, why Aunt Georgia had been so horribly afraid. It must have been because of this smiling man with a panther lurking behind his eyes, his smile, his mocking voice.

He turned into a little town, out onto a lane with a few

houses widely scattered, on farther toward a wooded section where there were no houses in sight.

"My pretty little Julie," he said, letting the car drop to a crawl, "I want to marry you."

She stared at him, brown eyes wide. There was nothing but intense incredulity in her expression. "Are you crazy?"

No amount of conceit could conceal from him the fact that she felt nothing but surprise and distaste. There was no trace of pleasure or gratified vanity in her manner.

He summoned up a laugh that had no amusement in it. "Do you think a man must be crazy to want to marry you?"

"Oh, don't be ridiculous! You couldn't possibly want to marry me. You don't know me. The whole thing is absurd. Now turn back—at once!"

"My, my"—he laughed to conceal his chagrin and his growing anger at her flat rejection—"you do have quite a spirit, haven't you?"

"Take me back to New York!"

He kept the car barely moving at ten miles an hour. Well, he had given her a chance to have it the nice way. If she wouldn't take it, that was up to her. He wouldn't bother to be so nice. "It will be a pleasure to break your spirit, Julie. I mean that. Break it like that." He snapped his fingers. As she reached for the door he stepped on the gas so the car leaped ahead. "Try to jump and you'll break your leg or your neck. You'd better think it over."

"You're crazy! Why are you doing this?" When he made no reply she clutched again at the door. Anything was better than this. Again he trod on the gas and sent the car careening around a curve so fast that the tires screamed. Like an echo, other tires screamed and a gray car rounded the curve behind them.

There was an explosion, and Norton's car swerved. He fought the wheel. It swerved again and began to thump along the road. He had a flat tire, apparently a blowout. He pulled off the road.

"One word from you," he told Julie, "and that will be the last you ever make. I mean that."

"Are you in trouble?" A car had drawn up beside them.

"Not at all, thanks," Norton said hastily.

Julie looked into the shadowed eyes of the girl who had seemed to haunt her for two days. She looked at the small, workmanlike gun in her hand with which she had shot at the tire. She spoke impulsively.

"My," she choked over the word, "my friend will have to change the tire and I have an urgent appointment. Can you give me a lift?"

"I'll take you back," Norton said.

As Julie slid across the seat and started to get out he grasped her arm, saw the gun held so steadily. He watched helplessly while Julie ran to the other car.

She paused for a moment in stunned amazement when she saw Bert crouching down on the floor, and then she got in, slamming the door behind her.

The girl at the wheel put the small gun in her hand-bag and the car moved smoothly off.

"Well!" Julie exclaimed as Bert climbed back on the seat. "I was never so glad to see anyone. But how did it happen?"

"Thought you might need a helping hand," Bert said. "You're all right, aren't you? We didn't close in until we thought it looked as though the party might be getting rough."

"It was! But what do you mean—we?"

"This is Jane Forrest. That was mighty pretty shoot-ing, Jane. What a gal you are!"

Something in Bert's voice made Julie look at him quickly. A little smile quivered on her lips. Whether he knew it or not, she needn't feel sorry for Bert any more.

"And now," she said, "tell me what this is all about."

XVIII

During the lull between appointments, Florence Gates had an opportunity to tell Princess Sobelli about her telephone call the night before. As she expected, the Princess helped her to prepare a purely fictitious report on her interviews, telephone calls and correspondence that indicated that everything was progressing smoothly and that the Princess was not getting out of line.

"How did they know that you were replacing May Williams?" the latter asked, "and find out how to reach you at home?"

"I discovered that without any difficulty," Florence told her. "I went to the file clerk, who was bound to have the personnel records and who would know if anyone had examined them. When I told her who I was she asked, quite openly, whether it had been all right to give out the information about me. A new clerk in the accounting department had come in and started to look through the personnel files and she had told him they were private because they contain the amount of salary each person gets, and all that, but she saw him take down my address and telephone number, and he asked how come the Princess had taken on a new secretary. It's just as well the department prepared all that material about my former employers and those recommendations."

"I'll have the man fired at once," the Princess said.

"If I may suggest, don't do that. We know who he is and he can be watched so he can't do any harm, but if they think we want him out of the way they will manage to plant someone else and we might not find out who it is."

The Princess nodded with a helpless gesture. "As you

like. Oh, sometimes I am so tired of this whole business." .

"It will soon be over, within a week at the outside," Florence reminded her.

"I mean the whole cosmetics business, having the big company with all its ramifications and its responsibilities on my shoulders. All the buying of materials and manufacturing and chemical experiments. The advertising and selling. The retail work and the shops here and abroad."

"But it's such a challenging business. Ever since I came in yesterday I've been wildly excited with its possibilities and simply teeming with ideas," Florence told her.

"Have you indeed?" The Princess's tone was curious, and the look she gave her new secretary was oddly speculative. "We must discuss this further when all the urgency of the immediate problem is over. Do you think you would like to stay on here and be trained to become, say, my assistant?"

"Your Highness!" Florence looked at her with glowing eyes.

"You wouldn't miss all the excitement of your present job?"

Florence Gates smiled. "I am engaged to a man who simply loathes all the danger and uncertainty in my present job. He'd love having me go into a peaceful field."

"Then we'll go into the matter later and see whether you would be qualified for the work." The Princess smiled at her and returned to her own office.

At six o'clock Florence Gates approached the desk at the New Yorker and left an envelope addressed to Mr. George Fairbanks. For a few minutes she stood looking around her idly. People were coming and going in the busy lobby, friends were meeting and parting, guests were arriving and taking their departure, luggage was being moved in and out.

A man was sitting near the desk reading a newspaper. He glanced at Florence and away without appearing to recognize her. A young man was standing beside a suitcase, a raincoat over his arm, a camera slung on a strap around his neck, obviously a sightseer who had just arrived in the city. Excitedly he snapped a picture of a movie actress who had just appeared.

Florence went out of the hotel assured that the letter would be picked up with competent witnesses, one of whom would record it by camera.

ii

While Florence Gates was leaving the faked report for Mr. George Fairbanks, Bert was ringing the bell of Mark Sefton's house on Gramercy Park.

When the two men were seated in the living room, Mark asked, "What happened?"

Bert described his activities of the day before and how Jane Forrest had told him about the three people who had trailed Julie.

"So they are really afraid of what she knows," Mark remarked grimly.

Bert went on to relate how he and Jane had followed Julie to the Colony and later had trailed her when Charles Norton picked her up in his car and drove her out to New Jersey. At first everything had seemed all right, and then Norton had begun acting in a strange way. He would slow down to a crawl and then put on a spurt of speed. It looked to them as though Julie was trying to get out of the car and he was making it impossible for her to escape.

"So," Bert went on, "Jane closed up, shot at a tire, disabling his car, and we took Julie in with us. Norton would have prevented her leaving if it hadn't been for Jane's gun. She's—quite a person."

"She's a whole army," Mark said. "Thank God, she was on hand. Did you find out what Norton wanted?"

"Julie says he tried to find out why she went to the Sobelli palace, what she was doing there. Then, all of a sudden, he asked her to marry him—"

Mark gave a sharp exclamation.

"Naturally she turned him down cold and then he got threatening. Said he would like to break her spirit. Then we closed in and brought her back with us. Took her home."

"How much did you tell her?"

"Just that we were keeping an eye on her. We couldn't tell her anything more. She's—she's so innately honest that she'd tell anyone anything she knows. We just didn't dare, but it didn't matter because she trusts me."

"I'm going to take over this assignment myself," Mark said. "How would you and Jane like to have a nice trip to the country tomorrow?"

"Suits me."

Mark dialed a number. "This is Mark Sefton, Princess. I know I suggested that we should not get in touch with each other but the situation is such now that I'll have to change tactics."

"What do you mean?" she asked in alarm.

"Is Julie there?"

"I assume so. I just came in myself, which is how I happened to answer the telephone."

"Will you please make sure that she's there?"

"Do you want to speak to her, Mark?"

"I simply want to be assured that she is safe," he said steadily and he heard her gasp. Then her muffled voice asked, "Perkins, has Miss Bryce come in?" Her voice came clear over the telephone. "She came home an hour ago."

"I want you to do something for me, Princess. I want you to send Julie up to your Westchester house tomorrow. Do you have anyone there to look after her?"

"Just one couple who stay on after Labor Day through to the spring. I don't really need a bigger staff in the winter as I rarely go there."

"If you don't disapprove, I would like to have Bert Wilson and a young lady named Jane Forrest, who is really one of our agents, go along for a day or two. Can they be accommodated?"

"Of course, but what is this all about, Mark?"

"Our friends tried to get hold of Julie today. Now that they have showed their hand they will have to get her, most probably as a hostage."

"Oh God," she whispered. "But suppose that Julie refuses to go? She seems to feel that she ought to stay with me."

"I will be at your house at ten in the morning with Wilson and Jane Forrest. Make sure Julie stays in until then. I'll carry on at that point and I will take her away if I have to handcuff her."

Even through her anxiety there was a lurking amusement. "I doubt whether you will find such extreme measures necessary, Mark."

iii

That evening Julie said nothing to her aunt about her strange and terrifying adventure with Charles Norton. Nor did the Princess indicate that she knew of it. But she studied her niece's white face and her lips tightened with anger. Her only comfort was her blind faith in Mark Sefton. He might be a disastrous man for her niece to marry but he would be a powerful watchdog. Julie would be safe with him.

It was a relief to both Julie and her aunt when they parted for the night. They had labored under such restraint that their conversation had been as artificial as that of strangers. The Princess, usually undemonstrative, gave Julie a light hug and kissed her cheek. "Sleep well," she said.

Three hours later, Julie repeated drearily to herself, "Sleep well!" She hadn't closed her eyes. She could not help thinking of Charles Norton, whose smooth compliments had changed so swiftly to menace. Of his fantastic proposal of marriage that was followed by his threat that he would break her spirit and like doing it. Of the unbelievable arrival of Bert with the girl named Jane Forrest, who had shot at Norton's tire and caused a blowout.

But neither Bert nor the fair girl who had been so persistently on Julie's trail would explain anything beyond the fact that they had constituted themselves her bodyguards.

It was daylight before Julie finally slept and she had just finished her bath when a maid announced that Bert Wilson was downstairs with a couple of friends.

Perhaps at last he was going to tell her the truth,

explain this nightmare in which she and her aunt were moving. Because the morning was chilly she dressed in a brown wool skirt and a yellow blouse with a matching sweater. She brushed her hair until it shone and challenged her unhappy face to smile. Then with her head held high and a smile on her lips she ran down the stairs.

Bert came to the door of the drawing room as he heard her feet on the stairs. "Hello there, sleepyhead. It's time to arise and shine. We're going places."

He drew her into the drawing room where she saw Jane Forrest, but a different Jane, a smiling Jane with a healthy skin and clear shining eyes, wearing a dark blue dress with a short wool jacket. Julie's eyes went past her, saw—

"Hello, Julie." Mark had taken both her hands in his and he was smiling down at her.

She found herself breathless. "Hello, Mark. What—how nice to see you!"

Bert looked from one revealing face to the other. "We've come to take you for a ride."

"Who has?"

"All three of us."

Julie looked in bewilderment from one to the other. Mark was still holding her hands. "You'd better have your maid pack a bag," he told her. "You'll be staying overnight. We all will. And take a topcoat. The evenings get chilly."

"I don't understand."

"We are taking you to your aunt's house in Westchester," Mark said. "She knows all about it and she has made the arrangements."

"But—"

"We're going to take you where Charles Norton can't touch you." Mark's voice was unexpectedly savage.

Julie met his eyes and slowly the startled look went out of hers, and she began to smile. "Right away," she said, and she ran up the stairs.

It was only a quarter of an hour before she came down to the elevator. Mark met her and took the weekend bag from her, put her coat over his arm.

"Where are the others?"

"Waiting in the car. Your aunt's car."

With one finger under her chin Mark lifted her head gently. "Today," he told her in the deep voice she loved, "I want to share with you. For one day let's forget all the horrors and be happy. Shall we?"

"I'd like that." Her eyes were steady on his. He took an impulsive step toward her and then he turned to open the door.

The big Lincoln had drawn up at the curb and Bert was at the wheel with Jane beside him. It was a glowing September day, with a chill in the air and warmth in the sun. The sky was a brilliant blue. All four were in a holiday spirit and they talked and laughed all the way to the big Westchester house.

The couple, Henry and Eliza Holmes, had prepared bedrooms for them all and waited to welcome them at the door.

The deceptive warmth of the sun misled them and they forgot the chill of the preceding night. "How about a swim?" Bert asked. "Are there any bathing trunks in the men's bathhouse or have they been put away for the winter, Julie?"

"No, they're still there. I have two suits, Jane. You could wear one of them. Let's go."

They put on bathing suits, Julie in yellow, Jane in blue, and ran out to the edge of the big pool where the two men were already waiting for them.

There was a sharp nip in the air north of Manhattan and Bert shivered. "I'm not so sure this is a good idea," he admitted.

Julie jeered at him. "Sissy!"

Bert laughed and dived into the pool. He came up with a howl. "Look out for icebergs!"

Jane followed and then Julie. Mark was the last. For a few minutes they swam vigorously and then they got out. Bert began to jog up and down the lawn to get warm. Only Jane, who unexpectedly turned out to be an expert diver, stayed in the cold water, but after a while even she gave up and she was content to stretch out on a deck chair in the sun, wrapped in a beach coat.

Julie and Mark sat beside the pool, talking so fast the words seemed to tumble over each other.

Bert looked at them and shook his head. "Eskimos," he told Jane sadly. "And here I am turning blue and no one cares."

"There are hot showers in the bathhouses," she reminded him and they ran off to their respective changing rooms. When they came out, fully dressed, warm and glowing from the exercise and warm showers, Mark and Julie were still absorbed in each other.

Bert paused beside Julie. "Pneumonia will do you no good at all, my girl," he informed her sternly, and Mark, aroused with a start, agreed. For him as for Julie it seemed that every moment of this magic day must be prolonged to the utmost.

Mrs. Holmes had prepared a delicious lunch, and the four young people had worked up a tremendous appetite which made her glow with satisfaction as the food disappeared.

For a couple of hours they sat or strolled in the sunshine through the big garden. Watching Jane and Bert, it seemed to Julie that she could almost see them falling in love. Each of them was able to supplement the other; Bert had a gentle undeviating honesty that was rare in Jane's world, and she had a fund of courage and daring that stimulated and delighted him. They would, Julie thought, build a good life together, the stresses and strains of their daily life compensated for by their peace and security at home and in each other.

She could not help wondering about Jane and what her real job was. A girl detective? It was possible, but somehow she did not think so. Something in which Mark, too, was involved. They would tell her in their own good time and for the moment nothing mattered but the moment itself.

When they went up to their rooms before dinner, Jane asked, "Do you usually dress for dinner?"

"As a rule, yes, but it doesn't matter. If you haven't brought a dinner dress I won't change either."

Jane grinned impishly. "Well, the thing is that I have a brand-new dress and I'd like to—"

Julie gave a gurgle of laughter. "See how it strikes Bert? Good! Come along."

Jane's dress was a filmy white that swirled around her

feet like foam. Bert, recalling his initial impression of
what she would be like, found himself staring at her,
enchanted.

Julie, in a soft yellow that brought out the gold lights
in her hair, found Mark waiting for her at the foot of the
stairs.

The evening passed in a kind of dream. Again they
ate superlative food. Later they put records on the hi-fi
and danced. It was difficult, seeing Jane, fragile and
dainty in her long white dress, dancing with Bert, to
remember that only the day before she had prevented
Charles Norton from keeping her against her will. She
wondered with a shiver what he had intended to do
with her. Jane was laughing up at Bert, like any carefree
young girl, while he told her one of his preposterous
stories.

Julie felt Mark's hand on her arm. "They won't miss
us," he said, and led her out on the terrace.

Now that the sun had gone down there was a sharp
bite in the air and Mark removed his jacket and put it
over her bare shoulders. He did not talk. He was content
to walk up and down, her hand under his arm.

It was Julie who broke the silence. "So you did come
back to me, after all."

"When I heard about Norton I had to take a hand."

The brightness died out of her voice, out of her face.
"So it was just for my safety?"

He turned abruptly, pulled her into his arms, pressed
his cheek against her soft hair. "Julie! My darling! When
I realized that you were in danger I had to come. Your
aunt understood that."

"You've talked to her?"

"Yes, of course. I arranged with her for all of us to
come up here."

"I wonder she permitted it. She doesn't approve of
you," Julie said.

"Doesn't approve—oh." His arms dropped away. He
released her and stood back. "We'd better go in. I'm
afraid you're cold."

Julie did not move. "Mark, I don't know what it is she
doesn't approve of, only that she thinks it is most unsuit-
able for me—for us—"

"She is quite right, Julie. There can't be any *us*. I love you. You must know that. I love you to the point of delirium. But I cannot ask you to marry me. My kind of life wouldn't be possible for a woman like you. I—for God's sake, there is a limit to my endurance!" He started to lead her back into the house, turned and caught her against him, his mouth covering hers.

For a moment of unutterable sweetness she seemed to melt into his arms. Then the door opened and the light spilled out on the terrace.

"Sefton!" Bert called. If he saw Mark's arms drop, saw him move away from the slim girl, he made no comment. "Telephone for you. It sounds urgent."

"It must be Aunt Georgia," Julie said in surprise. "Something must have happened. No one else would know that you are here. Would they?"

Mark did not answer. He had picked up the telephone in the living room. "This is Sefton. . . . At the airport! What on earth. . . . Yes, I came up here this morning. . . . The action is starting sooner than we expected. My God, I hope we're prepared. . . . Is Julian Thompson at the factory? . . . Fine, I'll be on my way to the airport in five minutes."

He put down the telephone. "I'm on my way, Red," he said to Bert. "Things are beginning to break at least two days sooner than we anticipated. I'm relying on you and Jane to look after Julie." Disregarding them he came to take Julie in his arms. "You are going to be safe, my darling, if you stay with Bert and Jane."

"And you? Please be careful, Mark, whatever you do."

"I'll be careful," he promised her.

There was a little break in her voice. "And you'll come back?"

"If you want me, Julie, I'll come back." He kissed her swiftly, got the car keys from Bert. "Sorry, but every minute counts. If necessary you can get a taxi."

"There's a station wagon in the garage," Julie said. "The Holmeses use it for shopping, carrying plants for the garden, that sort of thing. We can use that if necessary. Of course, the Lincoln is a lot faster."

Mark turned for a last look at Julie and went out. In a

moment they saw car lights move around the curved
driveway and out to the road.

"I suppose," Bert said, "we might as well call it a
day. But first I'll go around and check on all the doors
and windows and I'll spend the night on that couch in
the living room so no one can get up the stairs."

"You needn't worry about locks. The Holmeses are
very reliable."

"A little extra precaution won't hurt."

"All right. Oh, first I want to bring in the bathing
suits. I only have two and they won't dry in the bathhouse overnight. We may want to swim again tomorrow.
Shall I get your trunks too, Bert?"

He shivered ostentatiously. "Let it not be said that I
cannot die like a man."

Julie went out into the cool night air, her bare shoulders cold without the warmth of Mark's coat. The sky
was brilliant with stars. Overhead she saw the Big Dip-
per. Her heart was singing. Mark loved her. He was
coming back. Nothing else in the world mattered.

She walked along the gravel path to the women's
bathhouse, opened the door, and started to go inside.
Something heavy and smothering went over her head,
down over her arms, binding them so that she could not
move, she could not speak, she could not breathe.

Then someone was carrying her over his shoulder. She
was lifted and flung down on a piece of sharp metal and
blacked out.

XIX

By secret arrangement with Princess Sobelli, Julian Thompson was established as a packer at her New Jersey factory, where the shipment of heroin was to be delivered, transferred into other packaging, and sent on to be cut, bagged, and distributed. With a lawyer's passion for detail, Thompson spent an active day, unobtrusively examining the building from top to bottom, from the floors devoted to chemical experiments to those where cold creams, powders, perfumes, lip rouge, eye shadow, and countless other items were manufactured.

He checked the entrances, the windows, and the burglar system. In particular he studied the big shipping department where, presumably, the main activity would take place when the dope arrived and had to be repackaged.

To his satisfaction most of the employees lunched between twelve and one at the building's own cafeteria, so that he was free to make arrangements of his own.

He had been primed by an expert in the art of bugging a room and, before the employees returned to work, he had taken the necessary precautions.

He found the best places to set up a camera and conceal his own men. Three, he thought, would be enough inside, but for safety's sake and to avoid unexpected surprises, he arranged to have three more outside, in case they should be needed.

At five o'clock he picked up his jacket and left for the day with cheery good nights to the other workers. On his way out he encountered a big fellow who looked like a prizefighter. He had said that his name was Austin and that he was the new night watchman. Thompson eyed him thoughtfully. He would hate to have to tangle with this man, big as he was, because he would be out-classed. This was obviously the man who had been planted by the dope ring.

Hunched up against a wall, worrying about the possi-bility of a slip-up in the carefully laid plans, Thompson watched the employees leave for the day, saw their long line of cars move out of the parking lot. He had provided himself with a package of sandwiches and a Thermos of coffee. While he drank his coffee, he watched the lights flicker as Austin began to go through the building, osten-sibly doing his job as night watchman, actually making a thorough search. This was the time when Thompson began to worry for fear Austin would find that the shipping department had been bugged. Because he had once been outmaneuvered by someone who had moved before he was expected, Thompson was prepared to put his protective organization to work at once, even though his men would have to spend the next three nights waiting for something to happen.

At eight he heard a faint rustle and turned to wave to the three men who were to be stationed inside. Lights indicated where Austin was moving on the third floor.

"He'll have to make his watchman's report on the hour," Julian Thompson explained. "Then you are to go in and take your places. I know it'll be a long night but there's no help for that. Better early than sorry."

When Austin was at a telephone in plain sight of the window, Thompson pointed out the window in the base-ment which he had left open earlier and let his men in, moving noiselessly to show them that they were to take up their stations.

At ten o'clock he drifted down the street to a bar and grill that was still open. He went to the telephone booth at the back and dialed a number.

"This is Julian Thompson," he said when somebody had answered the phone.

"Thank God! Things are moving fast. We've just had word that someone slipped up."

Someone, Thompson thought gloomily, always slipped up.

"The stuff was put in the bottles at the palace on the day before yesterday and sent by air freight to New

York. It's due there anytime now and the fools didn't let us know. There must be no trouble with the customs men in case they haven't been briefed to let the stuff through. Did you get reinforcements in time?"

"I have all the men I need."

"We've informed Princess Sobelli and she said that Sefton was at her Westchester house. I just got hold of him and he's heading for the airport as fast as he can make it."

Thompson came back to the factory, found the three men waiting in the shadows outside, and instructed them not to show until they got his signal. Then he moved noiselessly toward the basement and the window he had left open.

He climbed cautiously over the sill. Before he could straighten up the big man had leaped at him. Thompson, coming out of a crouch, had time for one hard left, and then a sledgehammer seemed to hit him and he slumped to the floor of the basement.

ii

Julie's head ached horribly. She bounced around, knocking against sharp pieces of metal. There was a clanking sound. She was gasping for lack of air. In spite of her weakness, she managed frantically to claw off the blanket that had covered her head. For a few minutes all she wanted was to draw in the sweet cold air, to fill her tortured lungs, to breathe again.

Then she became aware that she was in the back of a pickup truck. She had been dropped on top of a tire iron. There were spare tires, a can of gasoline, a jack, and pieces of heavy chain. Apparently she had been kidnaped and was being carried off in a garage mechanic's service truck. One thing was certain: there was no point in trying to jump out while the truck was traveling at sixty miles an hour. She would never make it.

Then, unexpectedly, the truck slowed and stopped. Almost before it had come to a halt Julie had jumped off and started to run. There were pounding feet behind her and she was jerked so hard that she stumbled and lost her balance. She screamed in a frenzy of fear and a brutal hand covered her mouth.

"Oh, no, you don't! Stop kicking and clawing, you little wildcat."

She recognized the voice. It was Charles Norton, only this time Bert and Jane were not there to save her. No one was there to save her.

"I thought it was about time for you to come to," he said. "Another few minutes and you'd probably have broken a leg trying to jump off the truck and run away." With a swift, brutal move he fastened tape over her mouth, jerked her arms behind her and tied her wrists, drawing the rope unnecessarily tight.

He picked her up and put her on the front seat of the truck. Where was he taking her? What did he intend to do with her? Surely a trooper in a patrol car would see her, would notice the gag, would come to her rescue. Things like this couldn't happen.

"You've been a nuisance right along, ever since you started snooping at the Sobelli palace. Yesterday I offered you a nice way out."

Marriage with him, Julie thought. A nice way out. She shivered.

"But now you're going to be useful. Really useful." Norton laughed. "My ace in the hole."

Where were they? She had been unconscious for a while after he had taken her from the bathhouse in Westchester, but she had no idea for how long or in what direction they had gone.

Then she saw a traffic sign and knew she was somewhere in New Jersey. She was beginning to think more clearly. She could not get away. With her hands tied behind her she had no balance and could easily be caught by anyone. But she wasn't going to submit tamely. Whatever lay ahead, she would fight as long as she could.

Now and then she stole a look at Norton's face. He was not worried about her; his mind was intent on something else. He was slowing down as though uncertain of his way. Then he made a left turn and Julie looked up at the big electric sign over the building: SOBELLI COSMETICS, INC. It was her aunt's factory.

There was a truck behind the factory and the doors of the shipping department were open. Men were busy carrying in boxes and cartons while one stood guard, a gun in his hand. He turned sharply when the pickup truck came into the parking lot. Then he stared in bewilderment as Norton jerked Julie off the seat so that she stumbled and fell. He hauled her to her feet with a violent pull that seemed to wrench her arm out of its socket. Then he walked her to the door, holding her in front of him as a shield. "Just in case," he told her.

iii

The Lincoln sped toward Long Island—sixty, seventy, eighty miles an hour. A siren screamed and a trooper pulled the car over to the side.

"In a hurry, aren't you? Let's see your license."

Mark pulled out his identification and talked fast. The trooper nodded and opened a way for Mark who followed the siren, the speedometer leaping up to ninety miles an hour. At the end of the first trooper's district, another car waited to open the way through the night for the man at the wheel of the powerful Lincoln.

Mark was not worrying about the job at hand. The time for planning and worrying was over. All he could do now was cope with whatever happened as efficiently as possible. He was thinking of Julie. Julie who wanted him to come back. Julie whose warm lips had responded to his kiss. His heart sang. Even if the future held nothing else, he had had one golden moment. No one could take that away from him.

There were long lines of lights now and the constant scream of jets taking off, the roar of planes coming in to land. The tremendous traffic jam in the sky was worse than that on the ground.

He looked along the endless signs indicating the ways to the different terminals, found the one he sought, and pulled into an enormous parking lot, hoping to heaven that he was not too late.

He had time for a few brief words with one of the customs men, and then he caught sight of the truck with

its silver paint job and the words SOBELLI COSMETICS, INC.
At the moment the truck was unattended.

Then the action started. Three men began to carry
cartons and boxes out to the truck, working fast without
exchanging words. Obviously they were relieved to have
had no trouble with the customs men. They had cleared
their last and most dangerous hurdle without any problems at all.

When the whole shipment had been put in the truck,
two of the men got on the seat and the third climbed in
back. As he turned to close the doors, Mark saw the
bulge under his coat. He was wearing a gun in a shoulder holster.

Mark let the truck get far ahead of him. With its
height and light color it was easy to follow. He also had
the advantage of knowing where it was bound, so that
there was no necessity to close in.

The truck was sticking to a steady, leisurely forty-five
miles per hour. The last thing its three occupants
wanted was to attract attention by speeding. Thus Mark
sat relaxed at the wheel of the car. He hoped that Julian
Thompson had not been taken at a disadvantage by the
unexpected speed of the delivery, that he had had time
to make his preparations. Mark was not really worried,
however; Thompson was a man who inspired confidence.

They crossed a magnificent bridge, and Mark looked
out and down on an incomparable view of lower Manhattan and the dark Hudson with its docks and ships
riding at anchor. Another half hour and they had crossed
Staten Island, another bridge, and were running through
quiet streets in New Jersey, headed north toward the
Sobelli factory. The end of a great, complicated plan. If
they succeeded in rounding up the dope ring tonight, it
would be because of the assistance of dozens of people
in half a dozen countries.

A lighted church clock tower showed two-thirty.
Traffic was a mere trickle. Now the truck signaled for a
right turn. Mark waited patiently, giving the men time
to park beside the double doors of the shipping department and start unloading. He then pulled up to the side
of the road, locked the Lincoln, and went into the

parking lot. He walked warily, making as little noise as possible. What disturbed him was that there was no sign of the men Thompson was supposed to have planted outside the factory. One of them should certainly have challenged him by now.

But no one moved as he went around to the back of the building. Here light spilled out from the open doors where three men could be seen busily unloading the truck. Then Mark, lurking in the shadows, noticed the motionless figure with the drawn gun. Four men! Where had the other one come from? Something had gone wrong.

He went around the building, found a basement window open—how could Thompson have been so careless! —and climbed in. Not daring to risk a light, he groped his way around and stumbled over something soft.

Now, with a match sheltered carefully in his hand, he was looking at Thompson, bound, gagged, and tied to a pillar. Hastily Mark cut him free and removed the gag. While Thompson rubbed the circulation back into his ankles and hands, he cursed softly but fervently.

"What makes me so mad," he said in a whisper, "is that I told my men not to move without my signal, so here I've been trussed up like a Thanksgiving turkey and, of course, they couldn't come to find me. My own orders!"

"Where are they?"

"Three of them are outside."

"Why didn't they stop me when I came in?"

"Their instructions were not to do anything without my signal. They were to let anyone in, but nobody out."

"And the others?"

"I have three inside, hiding behind some large boxes and barrels of supplies in the shipping department. One of them is in a great spot to take pictures of the action. And, of course, the place is bugged. Anything they say is being recorded. But they, too, aren't to move until I say so."

"All right," Mark said. "So far nothing is lost. We're going to take all of them. Signal your men outside and let them close in." He smiled at Thompson's disgruntled expression. "Cheer up," he assured him, "we've got it made."

Thompson whistled softly and Mark heard running feet. Then, one by one, the three agents climbed in the window.

"All right," Mark said, "we've got them outnumbered. Five of us here, three more in the shipping department. Here goes." He flung open the door and shouted, "Take them, boys!"

Two of the three men who had been hidden leaped out, guns in hand. The third grinned as he looked through the viewer of his camera.

"You aren't taking anyone," Charles Norton said coolly from the doorway.

Mark stared in horror at Julie's white face. One of Norton's arms held her against him as a shield; in his free hand he held a gun.

"At the first move," he said, "she gets it." He jammed the gun against Julie's side.

Mark lunged forward but stopped short when Norton warned him, "Watch it, Sefton! This gun has a hair trigger."

Mark was motionless now, as were the men who had followed him into the shipping room.

"Take their guns," Norton directed the armed guard, "and stack them back against the wall."

Helplessly the government men let the guard take their guns and frisk them to see if they carried any other weapons.

"Now get that camera," Norton ordered. "Put it with the guns. If anyone steps out of line, shoot to kill—I'll take care of the girl."

"You can't get away with this, Norton," Mark said. "We have the goods on you."

There was a yellow glint in Norton's eye, like that of a wary animal stalking its prey. "Who's your boss?"

"The government."

For a moment the gun wavered in Norton's hand and then it steadied.

"Get on with it," he instructed the men who had been on the truck. "Get that stuff out of the perfume bottles and into our own containers. Austin brought the labels for the list of distributors with him and they should be all ready to put on."

"They are," said Austin. One eye was beginning to swell and discolor. He glared at Thompson. "This guy tried to give me a hard time."

Norton laughed. "Save it. You'll have your chance to even the score with him when the work is finished."

As Julie sagged against Norton's arm it tightened like an iron band. "Stand up," he snapped at her.

"If you hurt her . . ." Mark began.

"Cool it," Norton mocked him. "You can't touch us. You can't touch our organization. Before the night is over, you're going to surrender to me every scrap of evidence you have gathered against us, so that there won't be a shred of proof."

"You're sure of yourself, aren't you? You'll never get the evidence. That will go to a Grand Jury."

"Suit yourself, but I have the girl. Play the game my way or you'll never get her back."

But, of course, Julie realized, her heart cold, he would never let her go, no matter how much evidence Mark turned over to him. He could not afford to let her go. He had kidnaped her, crossed a state line. The whole thing would now come under the jurisdiction of the Federal Bureau of Investigation.

It isn't possible to believe that you can be killed. Even now Julie did not believe it. She looked from Mark, whitefaced and helpless, to his colleagues, unarmed and powerless, while the guard watched them, his gun unwavering.

Norton's men were working busily, emptying tiny slots in the sides of the perfume bottles, concealed by the clever design, and putting the powder that poured out into small containers, packing them in cartons, slapping on labels, working very intensely at top speed.

Now and then a late car went past on the side road that led to the factory. Surely, Julie thought, something would be done when the night watchman failed to report. Or had one of these men taken care of that?

Did the state police patrol places like this or did they leave it to a private watchman? Would someone notice the lights at the back of the factory and investigate?

Help had to come from somewhere. It simply had to. Julie, seeing Mark's concern for her safety, tried to reassure him with her eyes, as her lips were taped shut. Perhaps he did not realize, as she did, that Norton would never let her go.

For some time there had been no sound on the road, as though all traffic had stopped for the night. Then a car drove by, sounding its horn as it passed. Julie caught her breath, trying to signal Mark with her eyes. It had been the old-fashioned two-toned horn on her aunt's station wagon.

Julie's heart was pounding so hard now that she wondered if Norton could hear it. There was the tiniest flurry of sound, not much louder than that made by a scurrying mouse, and a flicker of movement. She caught sight of Bert's red hair as he peered cautiously around a big barrel and then dropped back out of sight. Then she caught the glint of light on metal. Jane had drawn her gun and was turning on the armed guard.

Mark's eyes were intent on her face as she raised her brows to signal him. She then moaned and slumped sideways as though fainting. As she did so, she caught Norton's wrist and dragged it downward so that his gun was pointed at the floor. At the same moment there was a flash and explosion. The guard screamed, dropped his gun, and grabbed his shattered left elbow in his right hand.

As though released by a spring, Mark was on Norton and had quickly and deftly snatched away his gun. His men had retrieved their weapons and were holding the drug runners at bay while Thompson snapped handcuffs on them.

XX

The telephone shrilled and Princess Sobelli, who had had it plugged in beside her chair in the drawing room, reached eagerly for it. She had sent Perkins to bed hours earlier. The whole house had slept since eleven o'clock except in the drawing room where she waited with Brooks Mansfield. Waited and walked the floor and listened for a car stopping outside, for the telephone to ring.

During that agonizing night she had told Brooks Mansfield the truth. She had agreed to work with the government in an attempt to trap a big organization engaged in smuggling dope into the United States. She told him bluntly why she had done it, that her husband, through no fault of his own, had become an addict and had died of an overdose of morphine.

"So I was willing to help stop this hideous thing if I could. I let Mark Sefton—" As Mansfield gave an exclamation of surprise she nodded. "Oh, yes, Mark is one of the government's star agents. This was his plan from beginning to end. He started the gossip about my business being in difficulties and staged that apparent insurance swindle when I claimed that my jewelry had been stolen. The idea, of course, was to make these people believe that I was desperate for money." She flushed deeply.

Mansfield was smiling. "Did you attempt to collect the insurance?"

"Of course not." She was indignant. "The insurance company knew all about it, and Mark has my jewelry."

Mansfield laughed. "Then what on earth are you blaming yourself for, my dear? You did a courageous and selfless thing. Surely you did not think I could blame you!"

"I didn't know." She leaned back in her chair. "But that isn't the worst."

"What is the worst, Georgia? Let's have it all."

"Without intending to, I endangered Julie." She explained the ill luck by which Julie had visited the palace at the very time when Charles Norton had unloaded the supply of dope.

"So that's what he is!" Mansfield exclaimed.

She nodded. And, unfortunately, Julie had not only seen the man outside the palace but she had mentioned it to him so that he knew he had been recognized. Norton had threatened that if she possessed any knowledge dangerous to him she would be killed, and it was no empty threat, because only the day before Bert Wilson and some government agent had saved Julie from him at gunpoint. The Princess broke off, her clenched fist beating on her chair arm.

"We'll have him arrested at once," Mansfield assured her.

"We can't do that, Brooks. What is at stake is terribly important, more important, even, than Julie's safety, because it concerns the well-being of so many people. Anyhow Julie is protected now. She is up at the Westchester house with both Bert and Mark to look after her."

"That sounds all right. Why are you so frightened?"

"Because tonight is the climax of the whole thing. The dope has arrived. It is being unloaded and repackaged at the factory now. If anything should go wrong—"

His hand covered hers, and in his warm clasp her tense fingers relaxed. "But Julie is safe and protected. You said so yourself. She will be all right."

"I suppose so, Brooks, but I'm afraid. I've been afraid for a long time."

He drew her gently to her feet. "Georgia, how much longer are you going to keep me waiting? Tonight sees the end of this long ordeal of yours, but how about mine? We talked recently about making one full life of two empty ones. Will you marry me, my dear?"

"Are you quite sure that is what would make you happy?"

"For ten years I've been sure that you were the woman I wanted. We have time ahead that we can fill with companionship and love."

The face that was coldly beautiful was familiar to thousands. Now, as the Princess smiled at Mansfield, few people would have recognized it. It had grown warm, the great black eyes glowed, the mouth was tender. He gathered her into his arms and for a long moment she rested against him. Then, as the knocker hammered on the door, she jumped convulsively and ran to open it.

Bert Wilson came in with a slight, fair girl wearing a long white dinner dress, the hem of which was torn and covered with dirt. The Princess looked at them, looked behind them. One hand crept to her throat.

"Where is Julie?"

"She'll be all right, Princess. It's over, all over."

Her voice rose almost to a scream. "Where is she? Bert, I thought you were guarding her."

"She was kidnaped by Norton but now she is safe. She's in the hospital," Bert admitted reluctantly, "but there is nothing wrong but minor things: a sprained ankle and a cracked rib and—well, it sounds worse than it is, but one leg was grazed by a bullet." The Princess moaned. "It's all over now. They will probably release her in the morning. But Sefton wanted to be sure she was all right."

Mansfield forced the Princess to sit down, and turned to the slim girl in the torn dinner dress. "And now," he asked Bert as he gave her a chair, "who is this young lady?"

"Jane Forrest, Mr. Mansfield. She's the government agent I told the Princess about."

Mansfield looked at the slight girl in surprise, but seeing that the Princess was wild with anxiety about her niece, he said quickly, "Suppose you tell us what this is all about."

Bert beamed. "Sefton called it a perfect operation. There are eyewitnesses, tape recordings, and pictures of every step of the operation from the very beginning to the end. Tonight at the factory all but one of the ring was photographed while packaging the stuff, their voices were recorded, and a list of their distributors was obtained. They will all be rounded up before the story is released. Perhaps they are under arrest already. And we've got Charles Norton dead to rights. He is facing a list of charges a mile long, including kidnaping."

"How could you let him get Julie?"

Bert's face flushed and then paled at the Princess's bitter reproach.

"That wasn't Bert's fault," Jane defended him. "It all happened so fast. She went out to the bathhouse to get the wet bathing suits and she—just never came back."

"It was Jane who saved her," Bert put in. "When we realized that she was nowhere on the grounds, we got the station wagon and drove to the factory. Jane shot at the armed guard and the whole thing worked out. It paid off in spades, Princess."

"Are you willing to swear to me on your honor that Julie is not seriously hurt?"

"Absolutely."

She relaxed and expelled a long breath of relief. It was Mansfield who said, "You say you got all but one?"

"All but the leader. Sefton has gone to take part in her arrest."

"Her?"

"Lady Maydock," Bert said.

When the exclamations of amazement had died down, the Princess expressed her warmest gratitude to Jane for having twice saved Julie.

"That's my job," Jane told her. "We wouldn't be here disturbing you at this hour, but Mark gives the orders and he wanted us to come here and report on what has happened at the factory and, of course, tell you about Julie. He'll be along later."

There was so much to say that the next hour did not seem long, even though it was a time of waiting. When at last the knocker sounded, Mansfield answered it and admitted a man with a white, strained face.

"Mr. Sefton! We have been expecting you."

Mark shook hands with him, nodded to Jane and Bert, and went to take the Princess's outstretched hands.

"Julie?" she asked.

"I've just come from the hospital. I persuaded them to let me see her. She is sleeping quietly. She'll be released in a couple of days but she will probably need a little time to recuperate from the strain."

"What about Lady Maydock?" Jane asked eagerly.

Mark tried to describe the scene. At Lady Maydock's hotel he had explained the situation to the appalled manager and promised to make the arrest so quietly that there would be no bad publicity for the hotel. Her residence would be referred to merely as "a midtown hotel."

Accompanied by one of his men and a police matron, he had gone up to her suite. She was awake, waiting for assurance that all was well and that the dope had gone off to the distributors without a hitch. She had flung open the door, expecting to see Charles Norton. It was obvious how she had spent the hours of waiting. On the couch there were strewn open jewel boxes containing diamond rings, earrings, bracelets, necklaces, which she had been fingering as a miser does his money.

In that first look she had seen the defeat of all her projects, had seen the prison doors close on her. For one wild, hysterical moment she had offered them diamonds in exchange for her freedom.

There was only one thing Mark did not tell them. Lady Maydock had looked at him and said, "Nemesis! I should have known, because I've always feared you. And yet, Mark, I came closer to loving you than any other man."

Then, with the fatalism of complete despair, attended by the policewoman, she had gone apathetically to her bedroom to change and pack a small suitcase. She had accompanied them without any disturbance to the station where she was booked.

"And that," Mark said wearily, "is the end of the story." He looked at Bert. "And the beginning of yours. Call your editor and get started, Red. This is your scoop."

Bert grinned at him. "Thank you. As a swan song it's going to be a lulu."

"Swan song?"

"I've been thinking about making a change, as I told you. In the morning, after handing in my resignation at the paper, I am going to apply for a job in your department. Will you put in a good word for me?"

"Better think it over, Red," Mark cautioned him. "It's a lonely life."

Bert grinned. "It doesn't need to be. There are girls who love that kind of life. Come along, Jane. See me write the year's best news story and admire me."

She smiled at him. "Stop boasting. You don't impress me at all."

"But I will," he assured her. "Oh, the station wagon is outside, Princess."

"So," Mark told her, "is the Lincoln."

"Don't worry about them. I'll have the garage pick them up in the morning. Good night, Mark. It was worth doing. I have no regrets."

When Mark had gone, Bert, who had just called his editor, put his arm around Jane. "Come on, Little Annie Oakley, we have work to do."

"*You* have work to do," she corrected him.

"But from now on it's your job to keep up my spirits and inspire me."

Mansfield looked after them, smiling. "There goes a happy couple. I was afraid Bert wouldn't get over Julie."

"Another happy couple," Georgia Sobelli said. "Now you must go, Brooks. There's so much to be done."

"Tomorrow—that is, today?"

"Well, in the immediate future. If we are going to be married soon—"

"And we are."

"I'll have to start training someone to replace me, and get clothes, and arrange—"

He laughed and kissed her. "Tomorrow is another day. We'll start planning then."

XXI

HUGE DRUG CACHE SEIZED, screamed the headlines, SMUG-
GLING RING CAPTURED. PROMINENT PEOPLE INVOLVED.

The story, originally Bert's scoop, made the front
pages of newspapers, it was prominent in radio and
television news, it was the sensation of the day.

There was a picture of Mark Sefton ceremoniously
restoring the jewelry to Princess Sobelli and a glowing
account of the latter's courageous part in baiting the
trap.

Julie, shut away in her hospital room, was sternly
denied any visitors, and the reporters and cameramen
who besieged the place were turned away.

There had been only one exception. Her nurse described to Julie the events of the night of her arrival
when Mark Sefton had disregarded all hospital rules
and insisted on seeing for himself that she was all right.
He had practically bludgeoned his way to her room and
he had stood beside her bed, the nurse said, for a long,
long time.

"If anyone ever were to look at me like that," the girl
said wistfully, "I'd be ready to follow him to the ends of
the earth."

Next day, among the flowers and messages and telephone calls, there came a box containing long-stemmed
red roses that scented the room, and a card reading:
"Wait for me. Your Mark."

The following day the doctor came in to smile down
at her. "Well, young lady, you've got a cracked rib and a
sprained ankle and you were grazed by a bullet. You've
been kidnaped and heaven knows what else. A very
adventurous young woman, if I can judge by the news
stories. But for some reason you seem to thrive on it.

We're going to let you go today, but your aunt wants to spare you the ordeal of coping with newsmen and giving interviews and being photographed. She doesn't dare come for you herself, because they watch every step she takes but she is providing a deputy. We are going to smuggle you out through the emergency entrance and you're to be taken to your aunt's house in Westchester."

"That will be fine, but I'll need some clothes."

"Your aunt has taken care of that, and everything you require will be sent up for you." The smile faded from the doctor's face. "You and your aunt are two very gallant women," he said quietly. "I've been reading of what the Princess did in order to help rid this country of those unspeakable dope smugglers. And from what I hear about you, you've had your life in danger a couple of times. And yet here you are, simply blooming. No bad aftermaths."

With the help of her nurse Julie dressed in a soft rust-colored wool dress. Movements were unexpectedly painful despite the rigid strapping over her ribs. Before leaving her room she insisted on taking the red roses. The other flowers, she directed, were to be sent to the wards. She cradled the roses in her arms as she rode down in the elevator.

Wait for me. She looked around eagerly as the wheelchair passed through the open doorway. Then she heard excited voices and Bert and Jane ran to help her out of the chair and into the station wagon. In the excitement of being moved and in greeting them, she managed to conceal her deep disappointment. She had hoped that it would be Mark who was to serve as her aunt's deputy. *Wait for me.*

Jane sat beside Julie in the back of the car and Bert took the wheel. He did not try to talk until he had maneuvered his way through traffic and was safely away from the hospital. Then he drew a long breath of relief.

"A whole bunch of those ghouls were outside the hospital waiting for a sight of you," he said indignantly. "They seem to have some inside source of information, maybe someone at the receiving desk. Anyhow, they knew you were going to leave today. They even set up television cameras." He chuckled. "They'll have a long wait." He added vindictively, "I hope it rains!"

Julie began to laugh. "This from you, the old newshound who made one of the big scoops of the year."

"That," Bert said loftily, "was a part of my hideous and now-to-be-forgotten past. May I have the pleasure," and his voice was formal, "of introducing that distinguished man, that prop of the United States Government, Herbert Wilson, Esquire, late of the *Sentinel*, soon to be the shining light of the Treasury Department. Eventually, no doubt, President of these United States."

"Conceited, isn't he?" Jane commented.

"So you've really done it!" Julie exclaimed.

"I really have."

"And," Jane added, "against all advice."

"Whose advice?"

"Well, Mark's, for one thing. He told Bert it's a lonely life. He said if Bert took the job he would have no time for love."

"Oh." It was a flat, dejected little sound. Then Julie recovered. "And what did you advise?"

"I advised against his making the change," Jane said seriously. "After that big story, his editor tried to persuade him to stay on and told him he had a real future on the paper. Anyhow, it was such a—such a safe job."

Julie smiled. "Is yours safe?"

"Well," Jane defended herself, "that's different. I happen to like excitement."

"So do I," Bert said. "In fact, I like trouble. I go out looking for trouble."

Seeing the glow in Jane's eyes, Julie exclaimed, "You two are engaged!"

Bert laughed. "I had to beat her into submission but she finally broke down and said yes."

Jane scoffed at him. "Finally! I like that. If he had waited one more day I'd have been driven to doing the proposing myself."

"She's a forward wench," Bert said, "but forgive her, because she doesn't know any better. And I took my time, I can tell you that. I've known her almost a week and I'm the cautious sort. I wanted to be sure that she wouldn't bore me in the long run."

The two of them poured out their plans. They were going to be married at once. Bert would give up his apartment and they would keep Jane's.

"That's really why I'm marrying her," Bert explained. "There's a big saving in rent involved."

He was not to report on his new job until the first of November, and Jane had been granted a leave of absence, so they would have ten days for a honeymoon.

"Mark arranged the whole thing," Bert said. "He recommended me to his department and they listened because they think he's a great guy. In fact, he is a great guy."

"Do you—see him often?"

"We're in touch but he is terribly busy, helping to line up all the evidence against Norton and his merry men."

"Not so merry now," Jane commented. "That's one group that is going out of circulation."

Julie tried to sound casual. "Did Mark know you were going to pick me up at the hospital today?"

"Sure. He's the one who suggested that we smuggle you out the back way. He sent you a message. Now what was it?"

Julie's hands clenched on her lap. Jane, aware of the mischief in Bert's face, which she could see in profile, wished that she could slap him.

"Oh, yes," Bert said, "he asked me to tell you that he is up to his chin in details, clearing everything up. He's leaving New York permanently, you know. As soon as his work is done he'll be seeing you."

"Oh." Julie could not restrain the brilliant smile of delight. He would be coming. Soon. *Wait for me.*

The Holmeses had the door open before the car had rolled to a stop at the Westchester house, and Holmes hastened down the steps to help Bert get Julie out of the car.

Mrs. Holmes was waiting inside to direct the men. "I've had Her Highness's little morning room on the first floor at the back turned into a bedroom for you, Miss Bryce, until your ankle heals. You won't have to walk upstairs."

She seemed rather disappointed when Julie refused to
be put to bed. Evidently she had looked forward to
nursing her.

Seeing that Julie was in good hands, Jane and Bert
kissed her good-bye and Holmes drove them to the
nearest station where they could get a train to New
York, a first step to marriage and the future.

ii

The ankle healed, and the cracked rib, and the gash
caused by the bullet left only a scar that faded from day
to day. And Julie waited. The days passed and then a
week, two weeks, three. A month had gone by since the
night at the Sobelli factory when Charles Norton had
used Julie's shrinking and helpless body as a shield.

After a Grand Jury hearing, Lady Maydock, Charles
Norton, and their whole ring had been indicted and
were awaiting trial. The distributors had been picked
up. There was nothing left of the whole criminal operation except for the heroin itself, which was ceremoniously and publicly burned.

Summer had passed, autumn had come, and that marvelous brief period known as Indian summer had
brought back warmth, along with a dazzling blue sky
and the brilliance of fall foliage, red and scarlet and
crimson, bronze and gold and lemon yellow. Sumac
burned along the ground, red ivy climbed a tree trunk
like licking flame.

Julie had long since recovered, but she remained at
the Westchester house. She knew that her aunt was
frantically busy, not only because she was to be the chief
witness for the prosecution at the trial of the smugglers,
but because she was training someone to replace her as
the eventual head of Sobelli Cosmetics, Inc., and making
arrangements for her approaching marriage to Brooks
Mansfield. She telephoned Julie every evening, discussing her plans, sounding as eager as a young girl. And
now and then she would mention Mark Sefton. She had
seen him or talked to him. As soon as he was free of all

his entanglements he'd be coming up to see Julie. Julie treasured every mention of his name.

Stretched out on a long chair on the terrace she looked into the glorious color of the woods beyond. Every year, she thought, I forget how miraculous this beauty is. As though every year, just before it goes to sleep for the winter, the earth gives us this wonderful promise of something marvelous to come, and to make us remember that, if winter comes, spring must be close behind.

There was something different about this day, something that sent a quiver along her nerves, cut short her breath. As though—as though, she thought, the time of waiting was drawing to a close. Or perhaps she was just excited because Aunt Georgia and Brooks Mansfield would be arriving in time for dinner and planned to remain for several days.

A car door slammed and Julie sat up, her heart thumping. Then in a few moments Holmes crossed the terrace. "A Miss Williams and a Mr. Turner."

For a moment, in her disappointment, the names did not register. Then she remembered her aunt's secretary, May Williams.

"Bring them out, please, and ask Mrs. Holmes to prepare tea." Julie got up to welcome the tall girl in the white wool dress, with its red belt, and the short blue coat. She held herself erect and walked easily across the terrace. This was the drab and colorless girl of a month before, this young woman whose hair shone, whose skin glowed, whose eyes sparkled. Automatically she pulled herself straighter as she walked, and Julie smothered a grin.

The young man with her had a pleasant face and an attractive smile.

"May," Julie exclaimed, holding out both hands, "how lovely of you to come!"

"Your aunt said you were well enough to see visitors," May said, sounding rather apologetic.

"I'm well enough to tackle a regiment single-handed and bored to death with doing nothing. You couldn't be more welcome."

"This is Paul Turner, a friend of my brother's," May

said. "He has just returned from Vietnam." Her eyes dared Julie to say that she had ever heard of the young man before.

"How nice of you to bring him," Julie said. "There's plenty of room here. Can't you both stay overnight, or even for a few days, if you're free?"

"Thanks a lot," May said, "but we've been prowling around New York for a week and we thought—that is—well, what we had in mind—"

Paul Turner took over. "The thing is, Miss Bryce, that since we both have crazy ideas we've decided to be crazy together."

When Holmes had brought tea, cucumber sandwiches, and one-bite cakes, Julie presided while Paul talked.

"You know," he confided to Julie, "sometimes in Vietnam I got to thinking that everything was sour. Then May's brother and I got acquainted and got to talking and he told me about his sister. We started writing to each other. From then on I had something to look forward to. So I thought it would be swell to meet her when I came home, because I haven't anyone here. But—" He shook his head in wonder. "But I never dreamed—boy! I never dreamed! Is she something!"

Julie smiled at his extravagant admiration. "You two make me think of those characters in Shakespeare who take one look at each other and fall in love. Not even an hour. Not a minute. One look."

"Why not?" May asked a little anxiously. "Do you believe it can't happen that way?"

Julie's color deepened. "No," she said softly, "I know it can."

"Well," Paul said eagerly, "you see we found out right away that we—well, we like each other a lot and we like the same kind of life. What we want to do is get married right away and spend our honeymoon looking for a place in Vermont where we can have a ski resort in winter and maybe hold local art exhibits in the summer. I'd rather use my severance pay that way and May feels exactly the same."

"And it's all right with the Princess," May said. "That new girl of hers, Florence Gates, is crazy about the job. In fact, she would like to study the business and work

into it, maybe get to be manager. So there is no problem. And the Princess said, when I explained that I was
planning to be married, that I could get anything done
at the beauty parlor that I wanted, and absolutely free,
as a wedding present."

Paul looked at her proudly. "As though you would
ever need anything like that!"

The eyes of the two girls met and they laughed in the
ageless conspiracy of women.

At length May looked at her watch. "We've got to get
back to New York. But I had to come and see you, Miss
Bryce—"

"Julie—"

"I had to come, Julie. I owe so much to you, so very
much that I can never repay, and I wanted to share my
happiness with you."

"Then that cancels the debt. We'll keep in touch,
May. And be sure you get that ski resort going soon,
Paul, because I plan to be one of your first guests."

iii

There was a chill in the air when Julie went into the
house. Holmes was in the main hall, carrying luggage up
the stairs.

"Her Highness has just come with her guests," he said.
"Dinner at seven-thirty."

Julie ran up the stairs, her heart thumping. Her guests?
Who, except for Brooks Mansfield, had the Princess in-
vited? She didn't approve of Mark so it couldn't be he.
Or could it?

She heard her aunt's voice speaking to her maid while
she dressed. It had never sounded so vibrant before.
Julie hesitated and then decided not to interrupt the
ritual of dressing.

In a slim, sleeveless violet sheath, her hair brushed
high on her head and falling in a soft cluster of curls,
Julie paused for a final look at herself and then went
across the hall to her aunt's room, the door now standing
open. The Princess wore a long dress of dark red velvet

that made her black hair and eyes spectacular. She was once more wearing her pearls.

She drew Julie into her arms, after a long scrutinizing look at her. "I've never seen you look better."

"That applies to you, too, Aunt Georgia. I can hardly wait to hear about your plans."

"Brooks and I intend to be married very quietly. There's been so much publicity about me. We'll have to wait several months, of course, to make sure that Florence can handle any basic problems. Later, I'll have to go back until she is able to make it on her own. Perhaps another year. But first Brooks and I are going to the Riviera for a month. All that worries me is—what will you do?"

"I'll be fine," Julie assured her. "I've been intending to go back to the New York house soon. And then I think it is high time I get an apartment of my own."

"But I don't want to drive you out. There is plenty of room. And Brooks wants you to stay with us too. Sometimes I think he is as fond of you as I am."

"I know, and I love him dearly too. But just the same, Aunt Georgia, I really want to be on my own."

Her aunt studied her and there was a curious smile on her lips.

"You mustn't worry about me, Aunt Georgia."

Her aunt's smile deepened. "I'm not worrying," she said.

When the two women went downstairs Brooks Mansfield was waiting impatiently in the hall. Julie held out her hand to congratulate him and then impulsively threw her arms around his neck and kissed his cheek.

"Welcome to the family, Uncle Brooks."

He beamed at her. "That's what I've been hoping, that we could all be one family."

Again the Princess smiled. "Perhaps Julie would rather have a family of her own."

Arm in arm with her aunt and Mansfield, Julie went into the big living room and stopped abruptly when she saw the tall, black-haired man standing in front of the fireplace.

She stopped short, her heart thudding, the beats seeming to tumble over each other. Then he came with long swift strides to take her hand and hold it in his warm clasp.

"You look—wonderful," he said at last. "What have you been doing with yourself?"

Waiting for you, Julie wanted to tell him. "Nothing much," she said aloud.

All through the delectable dinner Mark remained quiet. Now and then Julie was aware that his eyes were resting on her thoughtfully, but she could make little of their expression. Perhaps he had meant nothing at all when he told her to wait for him. Perhaps all he had in mind was to say that he would see her again some time. Perhaps she had believed what she most wanted to believe.

Her aunt and Mansfield were having a laughing discussion about a name for the house.

"Over my dead body," Mansfield declared, "shall it be given some cute name such as Cum Inn."

"And I'll fight to the death against calling it something ostentatious like The Manor," the Princess said firmly.

Julie began to laugh. "You know, it ought to be called The Ark."

"Why?" Mansfield asked her.

"Because they came, two by two. Today, Bert brought Jane; then May Williams brought her Paul; and now Aunt Georgia and Uncle Brooks. Certainly The Ark is the appropriate term in the circumstances."

"But what about you?" Mark said.

Julie had no answer to make.

When they had returned to the living room for coffee, Julie refused and Mark said eagerly, as though he had been waiting for an opportunity, "It's a wonderful night. Won't you come for a walk? Or is that ankle still lame?"

"It's fine." To prove how fine it was she ran up the stairs for a wrap and they went out onto the terrace, across the dark lawn on which the dry crackle of fallen leaves could already be heard underfoot. A full moon rode high and serene in the sky, throwing a white reflection on the water in the swimming pool.

"We stood like this once before," Mark said, "and looked at moonlight on the water. It was like a path on which we could stroll together." He reached for her hand, which had grown cold, and held it firmly in his warm one. "You know, in a way, I've been moonstruck ever since that night. That is why I haven't dared to see you. I waited until—"

She was staring at the moonlit water as though hypnotized by it; she did not look up. The color came and went in her cheeks. She wondered whether he could hear her tumultuous, telltale heart.

"A long time ago, I chose a strange kind of life, Julie, an uncertain and unsafe life. One which I had no right to ask a woman to share. A life in which there was no time for love."

As she tugged at her hand, he held it more firmly, ignoring its struggles.

"So then I found you and I fell head over heels in love with you. One thing was clear to me. If I ever let myself go, there would be time for nothing else. Just you."

She said nothing.

"So I finished the job I had set myself to do," he went on after a pause while he waited for her to speak. "Until I was free of all the responsibilities I could not say to you what I wanted to say. But I couldn't help—I did ask you to wait for me. I don't know whether you understood. I don't know whether I was a vain fool, a presumptuous idiot."

She was still silent but her hand no longer struggled in his.

"I haven't much to offer you, Julie. I've resigned from my government job and I am going back to my ranch in Montana. It isn't a plush life, and in some ways it's a tough one. But it could be good. It could be happy. I love you so terribly, Julie. Will you marry me and come home with me?"

She started to speak, found the lump in her throat too big to swallow. Then she saw his face, the sudden fear in his eyes.

"Have I asked too much?" he demanded. "Don't you love me at all?"

Still she could not speak. She groped in her small evening bag, and pulled out a torn scrap of paper, held it out to him mutely.

Unable to read it by moonlight he asked, his voice

husky with strain, "What is it? What are you trying to tell me, Julie?"

She spoke then. "Your telephone numbers. To call when I needed you. Remember? They've never been out of my reach since. I wanted—every day I wanted—but I had to wait. I had to be sure you wanted me."

"Julie!" It was a cry of triumph like a trumpet call. He opened his arms and she walked into them. In that warm circle of his arms she was sheltered and at peace. She raised her own arms and clasped them around his neck and lifted her face for his kiss.

After an eternity they were aroused by a wide stream of light slashing across the darkness of the terrace as a French window in the living room was flung open.

"What can have happened to them?" Princess Sobelli was saying anxiously. "Julie will catch cold. Oh!" As she caught sight of the man and girl locked in each other's arms.

Mansfield laughed. "Come back in, Georgia. They don't need us. Just each other."

Under the pressure of Mark's mouth Julie's lips were warm and soft. She drew back. "We'll have to go in," she said.

"On the ranch the nights are long and dark," Mark told her, "and there will be no one to bother us."

They crossed the terrace and returned to the living room.